EMILY RODDA

The Timekeeper

Illustrated by Noela Young

 Greenwillow Books, New York

Library of Congress Cataloging-in-Publication Data

Rodda, Emily.
    The timekeeper / by Emily Rodda ;
    illustrated by Noela Young.
            p.   cm.
    Summary: Patrick and his sister and brother are
    drawn into the desperate efforts to repair the
    Barrier between two parallel worlds before it is
    destroyed. Sequel to "Finders Keepers."
    ISBN 0-688-12448-8
    [1. Space and time—Fiction.
    2. Brothers and sisters—Fiction.]
    I. Young, Noela, ill.
    II. Title.
    PZ7.R5996Ti   1993
    [Fic]—dc20
    92-31512   CIP   AC

CONTENTS

Notes on "Finders Keepers"

By Max Treweek, Chief Computer Engineer and creator of the "Finders Keepers" television show, Channel 8, beyond the Barrier

As a child, though my first love was computers, I was always fascinated by the mystery of the Barrier, the invisible "wall" that divides our time stream from the neighboring one. At that time no living creature had been able to pass through the Barrier, though objects could slip through a tear or break easily enough.

From the objects that fell through the Barrier from the Other Side, it was clear that the people there were very like us, except for one thing. They were, it seemed, quite uninterested in possessions, and took no care to keep them clear of the danger the Barrier presented. Many precious objects fell through to our side each time there was a Barrier break. Even with Guards patrolling the Barrier's weak spots, and pushing things back whenever a break occurred, some "treasures" were always left after the break was mended. Barrier-combers (sometimes called "scavengers") would gather these up for sale.

I found all this very curious. Why did the people on the Other Side not keep their possessions away from the Barrier as we tried to do? And why, when our things *did* slip through the Barrier, were they never returned?

Years later, working (with computers, naturally) at Channel 8, the country's largest TV station, I got the idea that perhaps a computer could penetrate the Barrier and make contact with the Other Side. I experimented in my free time for years, and finally, after countless failures, I managed to create a computer that could do the job. I discovered, also, that by creating a link between my computer and a TV set on the other side of the Barrier I could actually bring people from that side through to this one, and send them back, as often as I wished.

The Channel 8 bosses jumped at my invention, when they heard about it. They needed a new, high-rating quiz program. Something different. And so the "Finders Keepers" game was born.

The idea was simple. Three viewers who'd lost something through the Barrier were chosen each week to be Seekers. Using the computer I would bring a Finder, a contestant from the Other Side, to meet the Seekers and appear to our audience. Then I'd send the Finder back to find each missing object in turn and win a prize.

The show was extremely successful. It was hosted by Lucky Lamont, a standard quizmaster-model robot. His minder, Boopie Cupid, proved very popular. She happened to be the sister of our canteen manager, Estelle Blacker.

The Finders answered many of my childhood questions. The most startling thing I learned was that people on the Other Side don't know the Barrier exists! There, it seems, the Barrier isn't a smooth "wall." It's broken up and impossible to see. When objects disappear through it, they're simply regarded as "lost." If they reappear, as they do if a Barrier Guard throws them back, people assume they simply didn't notice them the first time they looked. Hard to believe, but true!

I didn't have long with each Finder, because I realized fairly early on that it was dangerous for them to spend too much time on our side of the Barrier. They became weak and forgetful after a few weeks and began "fading away." This condition became known as the Trans Barrier Effect (TBE).

Our recent trouble began some months ago, when Boopie was showing her sister the "Finders Keepers" computer, which I'd stupidly left running in my absence. Somehow Boopie activated the program, and Estelle vanished to the other side of the Barrier, with no way to return or contact us. I'd always known that though people from the Other Side could move to and fro through the Barrier, this couldn't be done with safety by people from our side. And so it proved. The computer was severely damaged, and Estelle was lost.

We told no one. I worked secretly night and day to try to find Estelle and bring her back. But my every effort failed, and as time went by we became desperate. We knew that the Trans Barrier Effect would be damaging her. But in the meantime, of course, the show had to go on. And even that was difficult, because though I'd managed to repair the worst damage, the computer had become unreliable.

Then we had an amazing stroke of luck. A new Finder—a boy named Patrick Minter. His Seekers were Clyde O'Brien, a rather nasty fellow who'd lost a book in which a will had been hidden; Eleanor Doon, a rich old miser who had lost a ring; and a local Barrier Guard, Wendy Minelli, who'd pushed her boss's lucky toy rabbit through the Barrier by mistake.

Patrick was a champion Finder. He found O'Brien's book and brought it back. He then went after Eleanor Doon's ring and discovered that it had been found by his family's baby-sitter, who adored it. Patrick was fond of this woman. And he was worried about her, because she was pale, vague, and increasingly forgetful. He was right to be worried, of course, because the baby-sitter was in fact none other than our Estelle, who had by now forgotten about her past life, but who clung without knowing why to the ring that was part of home.

Patrick's a smart lad. Though he knew nothing of our loss of Estelle, he knew about the Trans Barrier Effect. He suddenly worked out, because of Estelle's condition and her love of the ring, that she must belong across the Barrier. And when he returned to "Finders Keepers" for the third time, he pulled her through with him.

So Estelle was returned to us. Boopie nearly went crazy with joy. But the effect on the computer, and on the whole Channel 8 power supply, was disastrous. Lucky Lamont blew up—on camera, unfortunately. The game was abandoned, and Patrick had to go home immediately, without the prize computer he'd been promised.

But that isn't the end of the story.

A couple of days ago Patrick found Wendy Minelli's lost toy and got it back to us through a Barrier break he discovered when his father "lost" his car keys. Boopie, Estelle, and Wendy insisted we try to push his computer through to him after that, and this, to my great surprise, we managed to do, with the help of an old rogue of a Barrier-comber, Ruby. I supplied a special contact disk with the equipment, so that we could "talk" with Patrick through the computer. This was a better idea than any of us knew, as it turns out. In fact, I'm beginning to think it might be the answer to everything. . . .

1
TIME OUT

When you're somewhere you don't want to be, a day can seem like a year. And four days can seem like an eternity. And Patrick really didn't want to be at his friend Michael's place, going home with him after school, sleeping in the top bunk in his room. He wanted to be home.

Normally Patrick wouldn't have minded staying with Michael. He wouldn't have minded at all. Michael was an only child, so at his place there was no little brother to pester you or big sister to complain at you and boss you. You could watch whatever you wanted on TV, without bothering whose turn it was to choose the channel, because Michael's parents had a set in their bedroom. Michael's house was big and new-looking, and very neat and clean. And Michael's mother always made a proper dessert for dinner—a pie or a pudding or something.

Most of all Patrick would have liked staying with Michael because of Michael's computer, and all the computer games they could play on it.

Yes, a holiday at Michael's place would have seemed like heaven not so long ago.

But it didn't seem like heaven now. Because now Patrick had a computer of his own. It had come into his life on Monday, after school. He'd used it exactly twice, just long enough to find out that it wasn't an ordinary computer. And then he'd had to go to bed. On Tuesday morning a grader working on the road near their house had broken a water main. There was water everywhere, flooding the road, pouring down the gutters—great! Patrick had gone to school laughing at all the people standing around looking, and the grader man explaining over and over again what had happened. He'd hoped it would still be going on when he came home. What a joke!

Well, the joke was on him. Mum had turned up at school with a suitcase at lunchtime and told him the water had been cut off to the whole street, and they couldn't live in their house till it was fixed. She and Dad and Danny, his little brother, were going to Grandma's. Claire, his older sister, was staying with one of her friends. And Patrick was going to stay at Michael's house. Till Friday. At least. Mum had said it as though she was giving him a present. She'd thought he'd be pleased.

He couldn't believe it. Of all the luck! All his life, practically, he'd wanted a computer of his own. Having turns at school or at Michael's place was okay. And sneaking into the computer shop up the road when the owner was too busy to bother about him was better than nothing. But a machine of his own! That was something else. And when he'd finally got one, he'd used it for one afternoon and one night, and then had to leave it.

He stood there in the hot playground and begged and pleaded to be allowed to go home. Said he'd look after himself. He'd keep the door locked. He'd live on breakfast cereal and sandwiches. He didn't need water. He'd . . .

But his mother wouldn't listen to reason. "Don't be crazy, Patrick," she'd laughed. "Don't be ridiculous! You can't possibly stay by yourself. And you can't stay in a house without water, anyway. It's not just a matter of drinking and washing your hands. The toilet doesn't work. What are you going to do—wee in a bucket?"

A couple of kids hanging around listening had giggled behind their hands. Patrick felt his ears get hot. He hated that. He'd stopped arguing then. He could see there was no point. In this mood Mum wouldn't change her mind.

So on Tuesday afternoon he went back to Michael's place. And Wednesday afternoon. And Thursday. Strangely enough, the days that he'd expected to drag had flown by. And now here he was in the top bunk in Michael's room, lying in the dark on the last night of his exile. Michael's computer sat on the desk, disks scattered all around it. And *his* computer was sitting in his room at home, waiting for him. Tomorrow he'd be back to it. Mum had rung tonight and said so. One more little night and one school day to wait.

At the same moment, not very far away, a nurse was

bending over a high, white bed, tucking in the rumpled sheets. "Go to sleep, now, dear," she said firmly, when she had finished. "It's very late. And no more shouting, please. You're disturbing the other patients." She clicked off the bedside light.

In the dimness black eyes stared at her, unwinking. "Then help me," said a frail but determined voice. "I must leave here. I am needed."

"Now you know you can't go, dear," said the nurse, impatience sharpening her voice. "You're very ill. You can't even get out of bed. Remember what happened when you tried before? You fell over, didn't you? Now please, please try to relax and go to sleep. There's nothing you have to do that can't wait. Nothing's that important."

The white head tossed on the pillows. The black eyes closed. The voice grew fretful. "You don't understand. No one understands. What am I doing here? How could this have happened? I must go! I must!"

The nurse sighed. Mad as a meat-ax, poor old thing. She turned and tiptoed out of the room, closing the door behind her.

Patrick lay back, his hands behind his head, and listened to Michael snoring gently below. It would be nice to be back in his own house and his own bed, too. And to see Mum and Dad. And it wouldn't really be bad to see Danny and Claire again, actually. They were irritating sometimes, but he was sort of used to having them around.

When he got home tomorrow afternoon he'd go straight to the computer and put in the "Finders Keepers" disk. Then he'd be able to get a message through to the computer on the other side of the Barrier, to explain why he hadn't been in touch for so long.

"Finders Keepers." Patrick smiled to himself in the dark. What a secret! What Michael would say if he knew! What they all would say! Mum, Dad, Claire . . . they'd flip! They knew he'd won the computer in a quiz game called "Finders Keepers." But they didn't have any idea that "Finders Keepers" was out of this world. Literally! That to play in it he'd had to cross an invisible Barrier, enter another time stream. That over on that side, in front of TV cameras and a cheering studio audience, he'd met three Seekers who'd lost a precious object that had slipped through the Barrier to his world. That *he'd* had to find these objects. Because he, Patrick Minter, was the Finder. And "Finders Keepers" was a sort of amazing treasure hunt, across two worlds. It was hard to believe, even for him.

But it was all true. The computer was proof of that, Patrick thought happily. He'd been a champion Finder. He'd found all three of his Seekers' missing objects. And he'd won his prize computer. And he'd made lots of friends.

Boopie Cupid the quiz show hostess, Max the "Finders Keepers" computer whiz, Wendy Minelli the Barrier Guard who'd been his favorite Seeker, old Ruby the Barrier-comber . . . and Boopie's sister, Estelle. His friends. They'd been through a lot together. He wondered how they were, and what they were doing now.

Patrick yawned, turned over on his side, and snuggled down under the covers. Well, he'd soon find out. In no time at all he'd be reading their messages on his computer screen. Probably they wouldn't have much news, though. After all, nothing much could happen in four days, could it?

2
SHUT DOWN

The late afternoon sun slanted through Patrick's window. He bent over and switched on the computer. Outside he could hear Danny chanting some kindergarten song as he played in the backyard with his latest obsession—a golf ball he'd found. Pop music pulsed dimly through the wall from Claire's room next door. Everything was back to normal.

The computer hummed expectantly, and Patrick sat down in front of it with a little sigh of pleasure. Carefully he slid in the "Finders Keepers" disk and listened to the soft beeping noises that meant the computer was working on it. Soon he'd be in contact with the people across the Barrier. Some of them, anyway. Max, for sure, and maybe Boopie Cupid. He waited for their first words to appear on the screen. He bet they'd be: HELLO, PATRICK. WHERE HAVE YOU BEEN? He'd tell them about the burst water main, and staying at Michael's place, and . . .

SYSTEM ERROR. CANCEL/OK.

He stared at the words in their black frame. What had happened? He clicked OK and waited. The SYSTEM ERROR notice appeared again. Patrick bounced on his chair in frustration. What was wrong with the silly thing? He canceled, restarted, and the same thing happened. He ejected the disk, stared at it, put it back. In seconds the dreaded black frame was back on the screen.

Patrick reached for the instruction book.

But nothing the book suggested made any difference. He tried everything, twice at least. Then he tested all the other disks in the box. Every one of them worked. He banged his fists on the desk. Somehow the "Finders Keepers" disk must have been damaged. How could it have happened? He'd been so careful!

Well, it had happened. That was obvious. Maybe it had been faulty to start with, or Danny had got to it and dropped it and had been scared to tell—something was just wrong with it, anyway. So he couldn't get through to Max, and that was all there was to it. Patrick stared at the empty screen before him and chewed his bottom lip. His chest ached with disappointment.

The door behind him opened and Claire came in. "This room's a pigsty, Patrick," she announced disdainfully, picking her way through the clothes on the floor.

"Yours is a hippopotamus-sty," he retorted automatically, without turning around.

She moved over to the desk and leaned over his shoulder. "What are you doing?"

"What does it look like?" Patrick wriggled his shoulders impatiently. "Get off me, Claire."

"Picky, picky." Claire tossed her hair out of her eyes and stared again at the screen. "What's the matter?

Can't you get it to work? Do you want me to have a go for you?" Her hand reached out.

"No!" snapped Patrick, and frowned as Claire jumped. He hadn't meant to be so sharp. "Thanks," he added quickly. "I'm just having a problem. I'll work it out by myself."

She shrugged. "Have it your own way. Look, I just came in to say I'm going to the shops tomorrow, and do you want to come?"

Patrick stared at the computer screen. Like I said, I'm having a problem, that's all, he thought. No point getting upset. I can work it out. "Oh, I don't know," he mumbled. "Which shops?"

"Chestnut Tree Village. Do you want to?"

"I suppose so." Patrick drummed his fingertips lightly on the keys in front of him, barely listening. He was thinking hard. The "Finders Keepers" disk was broken. So it had to be fixed, or he had to get another copy. And the only person who could do either of those things for him was Max. And Max was on the other side of the Barrier.

Claire shook her hair back again, and stamped her foot. "Well, don't say thanks or anything! One minute you're trying to get everyone to take you to stupid Chestnut Tree Village, and the next minute you act like you're doing a person a favor by going there. Make up your mind!" She flounced out of the room, slamming the door behind her.

Patrick sat frozen at his desk. Chestnut Tree Village! Yes! The only way to get in touch with Max now was the way he'd gotten in touch with him the very first time. Through the TV set in the department store at Chestnut Tree Village. That was where the link with the "Finders Keepers" program had been set up. And for three weeks in a row he'd gone to that one particular TV set, at ten o'clock on Saturday morning, and tuned to Channel 8. That had opened the way to the other side.

But would it still work? Last Saturday he'd played the

game for the last time. On Monday he'd gotten his prize computer. That was supposed to be his only link with the other side from now on. Max wouldn't be expecting him to make contact through the TV set again.

Still, with a bit of luck Max and the others might be wondering why he hadn't called them and might suspect something had happened to the disk. Then they might very well tune the "Finders Keepers" computer to the Chestnut Tree Village TV set again, just in case.

Patrick crossed his fingers. He knew it was a long shot. But he had to try. And tomorrow was Saturday, *and* Claire had offered to take him to Chestnut Tree Village. What a bit of luck! Shame he had been so ungrateful about it. If he wasn't careful, she'd change her mind.

"Danny, bath time, quickly!" His mother's voice floated up outside his window.

"Aw, Mu-um!" whined Danny below.

Patrick glanced at his watch in surprise, then looked out the window. Sure enough, the slanting rays of sunlight had disappeared. Already it was getting dark. The afternoon had flown by while he was puzzling over his problem.

But at least he'd made a plan. And that had made him feel better. Now there was only one thing more to do.

He switched off the computer, put his sweetest little-brother smile on his face, and went looking for Claire.

3

Three's a Crowd

"I want to go, too!" Danny turned down the corners of his mouth and gazed at their mother, Judith, with mournful puppy-dog eyes. He waved his spoon despairingly. "I want to go to Chestnut Tree Village, too." Cereal and milk dripped onto his sleeve, and he sucked at it absentmindedly.

"Danny! Don't *do* that!" sighed Judith, looking at him over the top of the newspaper. She reached for her mug of tea.

"Why?"

"Because it's disgusting, that's why," said Claire, chewing toast.

"Mum, Claire teased me!"

"Claire!"

"I didn't tease him, Mum. I just said he was disgusting."

"Mum, Claire teased me again!"

"For goodness' sake! Could we have some peace, please? Claire, just leave him alone, will you? Danny, eat up, go on now, or your Rice Bubbles will get soggy."

"Anyway, it's not fair. I want to go to Chestnut Tree

Village, too," whimpered Danny. "I want to see the clock and win a prize on 'Finders Keepers' like Patrick."

"The game's over now, Danny. And anyway, you're too young to play," said Patrick firmly. "And you can't come to the shops with us."

"Why?"

"Because you can't. You're too young."

"Mum, Patrick teased me!"

"Patrick!"

"I didn't tease him, Mum. I just said he was too young to . . ."

"Mum, Patrick teased . . ."

"That's *enough*!" Judith tore off her glasses and stumbled furiously from her chair, her red dressing gown tangling around her legs. She shook her fist at them. Her hair stuck up on end and her eyes flashed. The children regarded her curiously.

"You look like that sea witch on the telly, Mum," Danny remarked.

There was a short pause. Claire snorted with laughter. Judith stared at her reproachfully, then stalked from the room.

The three children looked at one another.

"What's wrong with Mum?" asked Danny. "Why didn't she say anything?"

"I don't think you should have said that about the telly show, Dan," Patrick explained carefully.

"Why?"

"I don't think Mum wants to look like a sea witch."

"Oh." Danny thought about that for a moment, then went back to his breakfast.

Patrick looked at his watch, jumped, and nudged Claire. "We'd better hurry!" he said in a low voice. "It's already half-past eight!"

Claire frowned. "It *can't* be! Oh, so it is . . . well, nearly. Your watch is a bit fast. Oh, well—"

"Finish your breakfast, Claire. We've got to get dressed and get going. We'll be late!" Patrick urged, still in a whisper. He didn't want to start Danny off again. Arguing with him would use up even more time.

"Late for what? The shops are open all day. There's no rush." Claire yawned.

Patrick didn't dare say any more. He glanced at the kitchen clock and moved the minute hand of his watch back three minutes to the correct time. He jiggled in his chair as Claire began buttering another piece of toast with agonizing slowness. Only an hour and a half to ten o'clock, and the bus took ages. Please hurry, Claire, he begged her silently.

"Hello, kids." Their father, Paul, wandered in and switched on the kettle. He looked around vaguely. "Where's Mum?"

"She got sad and went out," Danny explained, pointing with his spoon.

"Oh. Right." Paul nodded, and turned back to his tea-making. "Now look, kids, you'll have to be good and quiet this morning, all right? I've got work to do, and . . ."

"We'll be quiet. We won't be here. We're going to

the shops, so I can get a prize," Danny piped up confidently.

"That's good," said Paul, brightening up. "I mean, you know, that's nice for you." He began hunting around the kitchen counter. "Anyone seen the teapot lid?"

"Danny, we told you. You can't come!" exploded Patrick. "We told you!"

Danny drew breath, his bottom lip trembling.

"Listen, Danny, you'll have a lovely time here with Mum and Dad. *Someone's* got to look after them," soothed Claire.

"You just don't want me to come with you, Claire. That's why you're saying that," Danny quavered. "You don't care about me!" His eyes filled with tears.

Paul had been thinking quickly. "I don't see why Danny shouldn't go with you, Claire. If you're old enough to baby-sit for half the neighborhood you're old enough to look after your own brother for a couple of hours, surely." He gave up the search for the teapot lid and put a saucer on top of the pot instead.

"Dad . . ."

"Tell you what—if you take Danny I'll *drive* you to the shops. How about that? That'll save some time, won't it? And he'll be good, won't you, Dan?"

Danny nodded vehemently. "I'll be good! I'll be good!" he shouted.

"Okay, Claire?" beamed Paul.

Claire made a face, and gave up. "Okay," she shrugged. "As long as he does what I say."

"Yay!" squeaked Danny. "Thanks, Dad!" He gazed at his father adoringly.

Patrick groaned. Now he'd have Danny hanging around his neck, and it would be much harder to slip away to the TV set in the department store and try to contact Max. How unfair! He looked at the clock and jumped.

"It's nine o'clock!" he exclaimed. "Dad! It's nine o'clock! And you're not even dressed yet. If we go with you we'll be late!"

"Late for what?"

Patrick felt his face go hot. "I've got to be there by ten o'clock," he said. "I've got to. I . . . um . . . want to hear the clock strike ten. It's just . . . an experiment."

"For school?" Paul began pouring out tea, holding the saucer in place with one hand. Steam blew back and scalded his fingers. "Ouch!"

"Sort of." Patrick fiddled with his spoon.

"Oh, I know what he's on about," said Claire. She stood up, carried her plate to the sink, and turned to grin at Patrick. "It's because of last Saturday, isn't it? When the clock struck ten twice? Patrick, there's no reason why it should do it again this Saturday. That's silly!"

"That's not the reason," said Patrick with dignity. "I didn't even know it *did* strike ten twice last week." I had other things on my mind at the time, he thought. Like pulling Estelle back through the Barrier with me, for example. But come to think of it, that caused a real mess-up over on the other side. Shook up the whole

TV station. And the "Finders Keepers" computer. And the Barrier. Maybe it messed up things on our side as well. Made the clock go funny, for instance.

Danny was leaping and bounding like a puppy. "Dad, Dad, can we? Can we get there to hear the clock strike ten two times? Can we? Ple-ease?"

"Danny, it won't . . ." began Claire.

"Danny, you don't . . ." began Patrick.

"Danny, it's not . . ." began their father.

Danny's face crumpled. "Mum!" he called. He trailed from the room. They heard his voice echoing in the hall. "Mum, Mum, Claire-and-Patrick-and-Dad teased me!"

Paul sighed, rolled his eyes, and began swallowing tea, fast. "Come on, kids," he said. "Let's get this show on the road. I'll get dressed now and . . ." He noticed the teapot lid, lying on the kitchen counter by the stove. He shook his head. "That wasn't there before, you know," he said, almost to himself. "Definitely. Sometimes I wonder—"

"You're getting old, Father," drawled Claire. "Face facts."

Patrick grinned. He knew where the teapot lid had been. Through the Barrier, and then, courtesy of some efficient Barrier Guard, back again. His time on the other side had solved the little mystery of where lost things disappeared to, once and for all. He knew now that there was an invisible Barrier between the two worlds. And he knew that the Barrier sometimes tore, so that objects fell through from one side to another.

With his own eyes he'd seen the Barrier Guards on the other side pushing things like the teapot lid, and car keys, books, and even dogs' bowls, back where they belonged. He'd seen the Barrier Works Squad teams sewing up the tears so things would stop falling through.

They were well organized over there. There were even people called Barrier-combers who made a living out of picking up the things the Barrier Guards missed and selling them on little stands.

His friends over there, like Max and Boopie, couldn't understand why on Patrick's side people didn't even know the Barrier existed. But it was all very well for them. On their side the Barrier was easy to see—like a big, shining wall. And you could see the cracks and tears, and the things falling through, quite clearly.

But over here the Barrier couldn't be seen at all—it was too broken up and hazy on this side for anyone to notice. Patrick had thought of trying to explain it to his family—of course he had. But somehow he knew they wouldn't believe him. Well, Danny might. But Danny would believe anything. He didn't count.

Thinking of Danny brought Patrick back to the present. Just for once Danny had been quite useful. Thanks to him, things were at last going Patrick's way. He'd be at the TV set in Chestnut Tree Village by ten o'clock now for sure. And then—well, only time would tell what would happen next.

4

CONTACT

As soon as Paul dropped them off, Patrick could see that he wasn't the only one in a hurry at Chestnut Tree Village. On the ground floor, where they went in, it was very busy indeed. People were bustling around, pushing their way around the queues that had formed in front of the food counters, while the shop assistants rushed to and fro pushing things into bags, grabbing money, and thrusting back the change.

"Aren't they slow? And I'm that late! I don't know where the time's gone this morning!" they heard an old woman complain to the man next to her.

"You and me both," he grunted, pulling at his mustache and looking off into the distance.

"It's been like it all week, really," the old lady chatted on. "It's flown! It'll be Christmas before we know it. I was saying to my husband only yesterday, it'll be Christmas . . ."

Patrick and Claire made for the escalators. "Claire, wait!" Danny's voice wailed faintly behind them. "Claire!" Claire looked around, exclaimed and plunged back into the small crowd milling in front of a fruit counter. She emerged dragging a pink-faced Danny by the hand. "Keep up," she scolded.

"I dropped my golf ball," he explained, showing her. "And you didn't wait!"

Patrick sighed. "I told you not to bring that, Danny. I *told* you! You'll just lose it. Put it back in your pocket." He glanced at his watch. A quarter to ten. "Come *on!*" he shouted.

The escalators were crowded with people. The children stood hemmed in as they moved slowly up to the next level.

"We'll miss the clock," worried Danny, jiggling impatiently. "We'll miss it going twice!"

Patrick saw the woman on the step below them smile. "Sshh!" he hissed, embarrassed. "We've got plenty of time. It'll be all right." I hope, he thought, gritting his teeth.

They reached the top level at last. Danny bolted for the clock, which stood in the center of the floor surrounded by its little white fence and a neat row of bushes in pots. Patrick followed with Claire, trying not to look too eager. He glanced at his watch. Ten minutes to ten. The escalators really had been slow. But still, as he'd said to Danny, there was plenty of time. His heart was thumping. In fact, he had to kill time, he decided, until Claire was firmly trapped with Danny at the clock and he could get away.

He left her side and strolled over to the antique shop window, pretending to look at the display. But his eyes flicked around, barely noticing the shining silver, the painted ornaments, and the brightly colored hummingbirds in their glass case. Claire was staring at him. He could feel it. He resisted the urge to look at his watch again and pretended instead to read the gold lettering at the bottom of the shop window. A. V. VARGA, PROPRIETOR. He nodded as if this was important.

"Come on, Patrick," Claire called from across the plaza. Reluctantly he wandered over to join her.

As usual a small crowd had gathered by the fence to watch the clock strike. Small children and their parents, talking, pointing, and excited; interested adults, and kids as old as Patrick or older, pretending they just happened to be passing. In a few minutes the blacksmith would begin to swing his hammer to strike the hour on his anvil. Then the little birds would pop out of holes in the chestnut tree's branches, the painted, smiling sun would rise behind the leaves, and a squirrel would peep out of the tree trunk. It was an extraordinary clock, all right. Patrick wondered who had made it.

He reached the fence and watched Danny wriggle into place right under the front of the clock, where he could clearly see the hands. Soon he would have to make some excuse to wander off to the department store and get to the TV set that was his contact point with Max.

"You know, they should look after this thing better," said Claire disapprovingly, coming up behind him. "Look, the paint's peeling off and everything."

Patrick looked, and frowned in surprise. Claire was right. Spots of paint had come off some of the green leaves. And the blacksmith's carved arm had a crack in

it. He hadn't noticed that before. He leaned over the fence to look more closely, pushing aside the branches of one of the potted plants as he did so. And then he saw. The paint wasn't peeling. It had been chipped off. And the crack in the blacksmith's arm looked very new.

"Patrick, for heaven's sake, get out of there," said Claire, pulling at his arm. "You'll wreck the plant!" She began fussing with the floppy, bent branches, and then stopped and stared. "Oh, look at *this*!" She pushed him out of the way and plunged her hand into the flowerpot, bringing up a blue-and-yellow object that had lain hidden there.

"It's one of the birds off the clock." She held it out for him to see. "It must have fallen off into the pot." She looked up, pointing. "Yes, it must have come out of the hole up there. Gosh, it's heavy—it's made of china or something. Lucky it didn't break. Poor little bird. Isn't that awful?"

"Let me see!" Patrick held out his hand, but Claire's fingers closed protectively over her find.

"I'll hand it in on the way out," she said, pushing the bird into her shoulder bag. "You better not touch it. You might break it."

"Claire, don't be . . ."

"Claire—Patrick—quick, quick! Look!" Danny was jumping up and down, shouting at them from his place in front of the clock. "It's going to go!"

"Not for a little while, Danny," called Claire. She glanced at her watch. "Seven minutes to wait!"

"No, no," called Danny. "Look! *Look*, Claire!" He pointed urgently.

Claire and Patrick glanced at each other, sighed, and shook their heads. Kids! They walked around the fence till they stood by Danny's side, facing the clock.

"See!" he chortled triumphantly, grabbing Claire's hand. "I *told* you, Claire!"

"It's fast!" exclaimed Claire in astonishment. "How about that!"

It was true. The hands of the clock were pointing at two minutes to ten. Claire and Patrick looked at their watches and then at each other. Patrick's stomach turned over. The Chestnut Tree Village clock was never ever wrong. But today it was. It was five minutes fast. No doubt about it. He thought quickly. What did this mean? Would the "Finders Keepers" channel open when the clock chimed, as it had before? Or at the real ten o'clock? He didn't know, and he couldn't risk a mistake. He'd have to go get to the TV set now.

"Told you!" repeated Danny. He tightened his grip on Claire's hand and, with a sigh of satisfaction, leaned on the fence, his eyes fixed on the place where the squirrel usually appeared.

"Claire—I've, um, just got to go somewhere," murmured Patrick, backing away quickly through the crowd. "I'll be back in a minute. Okay?"

"What do you mean, you've got to go somewhere?" demanded Claire. She twisted around, trying to see her brother, but he had already disappeared from view. "Patrick, I thought you wanted to see . . . Patrick!

Come back here!" she called. She met the amused eyes of the woman behind her, forced a smile, and turned as casually as she could back to Danny. How embarrassing!

Patrick half ran to the department store entrance and down the line of TV sets till he reached the one he had used before. It was on. He switched rapidly to Channel 8. Roaring snow filled the screen. Patrick leaned forward tensely, waiting. His ears strained for the sound of the clock.

And then he heard it—its chime louder and more grating than he remembered. *One . . . two . . .*

The screen flickered. A moving shadow appeared in its center, dotted and surrounded by dancing points of light. Patrick tried to make out what it was. The shadow moved; its shape became clearer. It was a face. It was Max! His mouth was moving, as if he was shouting, but Patrick could hear nothing above the roaring of the snow.

Four . . . five . . . chimed the clock.

"Max!" yelled Patrick. "Max, it's me, Patrick! I need your help!"

"Help. . . ." Was that an echo of his own voice, bouncing back to him, or was it . . . ?

Six . . .

The image on the screen wavered. Patrick watched helplessly. What was Max trying to say? What should he do?

Seven . . . eight . . .

Patrick shut his eyes, put his hand over one ear, and

pressed his other ear against the TV screen. He held his breath.

Nine . . .

Max's voice, faint, tinny, and distorted, but filled with urgency, finally penetrated the background roar. "Need help. . . . Will you come?"

"*Yes!*" Patrick shouted. And the blackness closed in.

"The clock! I must . . . quickly . . . no time!" The old woman struggled to sit up, fell back on the starched pillows. A plump, pink-uniformed figure stood gaping at her, a cup of tea in one hand. The old woman beat her small fists feebly on the sheets. "The clock! Do something, you fool!"

"Well, honestly," sniffed the person in pink. Then she stiffened in alarm. The woman in the bed was clutching at her chest, panting for breath. "I'll get a doctor! Hold on!" She made for the door, slopping tea as she ran.

"Fool!" The woman in the bed tossed her white head from side to side. "There's no time for that! No time . . ."

5

Behind the Barrier

A roaring sound filled Patrick's ears. His stomach churned. His side ached. What had happened? He realized that his hands were pressed against his eyes, and slowly he forced himself to pull them away. He blinked, unable at first to believe what he was seeing.

He was lying on the ground, outside, in open air, next to a high wire fence. People stumbled and shouted around him, buffeted by the roaring wind, lurching as the earth rumbled and trembled. Patrick staggered to his feet, wincing with pain. He must have landed heavily and hurt himself. He shook his head, trying to clear it. Where was Max? And the TV studio? Where was he?

He looked around. And slowly he realized where he was. He had been here before. He was down by the Barrier, where Wendy Minelli, the Barrier Guard, had her post. But it all looked different. This fence—it was new. A whole section of the shimmering Barrier had been fenced off. Instead of one or two red-coated Guards patrolling the Barrier, now there were dozens running and jostling in panic, being shouted at by big, tall men and women in shiny black uniforms and peaked hats who seemed to be in charge. High scaffolding had been built against the Barrier itself. All over the scaffolding hung Barrier Works Squad staff, sturdy in their red overalls and yellow crash helmets, battling against the howling wind, working away with their needles and thread for dear life.

Patrick could see why. There was a huge Barrier break going on in the fenced-off area. Behind the scaffolding, black tears crisscrossed the shining Barrier surface, and through the holes poured a flood of things from the other side—bicycles and shoes, books and hammers and watering cans, hats and sweaters and keys and jewelry, and, of course, a perfect flurry of odd socks. As fast as the Barrier Guards threw things back, more fell through. And as fast as the Barrier Works Squad mended the tears, more tears appeared.

"Let us through, you mongrels!" shrieked a voice beside Patrick. He looked around fearfully. A ragged man, his glittering eyes fixed on the Barrier, was shaking his fist at the Guards and their black-clad bosses. "Let us through!" the man yelled again, and kicked at the fence furiously. "We've got a right! Scavengers' rights! We've got a right to the pickings! Let us through!"

"Yeah!" another voice shouted. "We've got our living to make, haven't we? Let us through!"

"Let us through! Let us through!" The angry call was taken up by Barrier-combers all along the fence. The people in front began to kick the wire. The people behind pushed forward. The fence began to bend. Patrick stared around him, with a rising feeling of panic. There were so many people. He was pressed tightly against the wire. What was going to happen? If the fence collapsed, he'd be trampled. He saw one of the black-uniformed people down by the Barrier look up toward them. She reacted quickly, pointing and barking orders to five or six others, who began running toward the fence, pulling shining black sticks from their belts.

Patrick began to push and shove, too, desperately trying to wriggle back through the crowd, away from the fence. The Barrier-combers hardly looked at him. They had other things on their minds. The black guards reached the fence and silently took their places along it, tall and menacing, brandishing their weapons in gloved hands. Their faces were grim, their eyes hidden behind shining black wraparound sunglasses.

They looked terrifying to Patrick, but the Barrier-combers were unimpressed.

"Aren't they the cuties, in their little black boots and all?" shrilled one. "Give us a kiss, dear!"

"Why did the Agent cross the road?" called another voice.

"I don't know, Sam," shrieked another. "Why did the Agent cross the road?"

"To beat up the chicken on the other side, of course."

"Ha, ha, ha!" roared the Barrier-combers. The black figures raised their weapons a little higher.

Patrick had had enough. He put his head down and pushed with all his might, boring through the grunting, complaining press of people, refusing to give up. All he knew was that he had to get away from the fence. Before the Barrier-combers made another try for the Barrier. Before the Agents, or whatever they were called, got really irritated and decided to charge.

He reached the back of the crowd, made a final enormous effort, and popped out of the mass of bodies like a cork out of a bottle, catapulting straight into something soft.

"Oof!" gasped the something, staggering. "Hey, watch it, will you?"

Patrick raised his head. He couldn't believe his luck. "Ruby!" he shouted, over the raging wind. "Oh, Ruby!"

"Well, blow me down." The old Barrier-comber rubbed her stomach and looked down at him in astonishment. "It's the little bloke from the other side. Patrick, isn't it? What're you doing back again?"

"Max called me," said Patrick. "Ruby, what's happening?"

There was a crack that sounded like thunder and a roar from the crowd behind them. Ruby's white hair and tattered clothes flapped around her in the wind. She frowned at Patrick and shook her head. "I've never seen anything like it," she said. "Never in all my years on the Barrier. It's like the thing's breaking apart. They can't stop it. It's been going on for a week, getting worse and worse. The Guards and the Works Squads couldn't cope, so yesterday the National Agents were sent in. They're supposed to be disaster experts. Huh! They put up that fence to keep us out and they've been marching up and down giving orders and messing everyone around. But as far as the Barrier's concerned they're

about as much use as a pocket in a singlet. Poor
Wendy's that upset. This is her beat. She feels responsi-
ble, see. She's working herself into the ground. I said
to her, 'Wendy, you'll kill yourself if you don't—'"

"But Ruby," interrupted Patrick. "What's caused it?
Why's it happening?"

Ruby looked around nervously. She bent toward
him. "On the news they say it's all quite natural and
not to worry, it'll fix itself up and all that stuff," she
said in his ear. "But around here a lot of people
reckon . . ." She broke off. A lone Barrier-comber was
passing, looking at them curiously. Patrick stared back
at her. She seemed familiar. Her hollow eyes were
piercing. Her mouth moved, and she dabbed at it with
a grimy handkerchief. On her bony fingers dozens of
rings glittered.

Patrick jumped. Of course! Of course he had seen
this woman before. She was Eleanor Doon, one of the
Seekers he had played for in "Finders Keepers." But
what was she doing here? She'd gotten her ring back.
He had found it for her. So . . .

He glanced at Ruby and was startled to see that her
weather-beaten face had paled and she was staring
fixedly at Eleanor Doon.

"Ruby, what's the matter?" asked Patrick.

"Don't say anything!" she whispered, pulling him
closer to her. Patrick struggled a little, confused and
frightened, but her hand was like iron on his arm. In
grim silence she wrapped one side of her floppy green
cardigan around his head and shoulders and pulled it

tight, so that he was partly hidden against her body. Then she began walking rapidly up the hill, with Patrick stumbling beside her. "What an old fool!" he heard her muttering to herself as she strode along. "What a fool! Where's your brains, Ruby? Chatting away like it's a tea party. A half-trained penguin'd know better. . . ."

She's crazy, Patrick thought. What'll I do? I've got to get away! But Ruby was too strong for him. He staggered blindly along, half suffocated by the musty smell of the cardigan that bound him, hearing only her muttering, the thudding of his own heart, and the roaring of the wind.

"Aha!" The old woman stopped with a jerk. Patrick made an effort to pull himself free, but she gripped him even more tightly. "Quiet!" she wheezed fiercely. "If you know what's good for you!"

They stood still, panting, while the wind howled around them. Behind them, faintly now, rose the sound of the Barrier-combers chanting. Then Patrick heard a shout and the sound of feet thudding toward them. Again he struggled to free himself, and again Ruby's arm gripped him and forced him to be still.

The feet stopped in front of them.

"Ruby!" squeaked a familiar voice. "Have you . . . ?" Patrick's heart leaped.

"I've got him," Ruby said. "Now, you two just get him out of here!" Her fierce grip loosened and, gasping and crying with relief, Patrick darted out of the stifling folds of her cardigan and into the waiting arms of Boopie Cupid.

6

BAN THE FINDERS!

"Sweetie pie, oh dear, are you all right?" Boopie Cupid patted Patrick's shaking shoulders. "The computer's haywire, isn't it, Max? But we *never* thought it'd dump you out here instead of inside. Or we'd never have brought you over. I'm so sorry. Thank heavens Ruby found you. We've been looking everywhere for you, haven't we, Max?"

Max nodded. He looked worried and ill.

"Listen, don't waste time yapping now," urged Ruby. She glanced behind her. "That crazy Seeker of yours—you know, the Doon woman whose ring Patrick found on the show—she was here. She saw Patrick. If she notices who he is and blabs, there'll be a riot!"

Boopie clutched Patrick more tightly. "What on earth was Eleanor Doon doing here? She got her ring back. Don't say she's lost something else!"

Ruby snorted. "Oh, she started hanging round the Barrier months ago. Looking for the ring, I s'pose. A few Barrier-combers start off like that. The amateurs, that is." She looked behind her again and rushed on. "They come down to the Barrier one day, looking for something they've lost, see? And along the way they find a few other things. Well, some of them get to like the idea. And they come back the next day, and the next, and after a while, even if they've found the thing they lost in the first place, they can't stay away. They get sort of hooked. Something for nothing, see? They can't resist it, even when they're rich, like Loony Doon. They're a pain in the neck. They get in the way—and for what? It's not a business for them, see, like it is for us professionals."

The old woman drew herself up, wrapping her cardigan more tightly around her as the wind whipped her white hair into tangles. "They don't sell the stuff. They don't even give it away. They just take it home and keep it, like poor old dogs burying bones. It's a disease with them. And a wicked waste of good stuff. I reckon they should be banned, for their own good and everyone else's."

Max was hardly listening. His eyes were fixed on the scene in the valley below them. "Boopie, look at the Barrier," he said.

Boopie looked, and her hand flew to her mouth. "It's worse. Oh, Max, it's worse!"

"Getting worse all the time," said Ruby. She looked sharply at Max. "You know what they're saying, don't you?"

He nodded.

"It's stupid!" Boopie burst out. "They don't know what they're talking about!"

"Well, be that as it may," croaked Ruby, pursing her lips, "they're pretty het up. And I don't blame them. I don't swallow all that guff about natural disaster and whatnot. I mean, if it's so natural, why hasn't it happened before? And why's it going on so long? And if it's not natural, what is it?" She rounded on Max. "You're the genius! Do *you* know?"

Max's shoulders sagged. He looked very tired. "I've got an idea," he said. "But I can't be sure . . ." He glanced at Patrick, and his voice strengthened. "That's why Patrick's here, actually," he said. "He's going to help."

"Him?" Ruby exploded. "The kid? Well, look, if that's your best offer, I think we'd all better pack our bed socks and start running!" She nodded quickly at Patrick. "No offense, sonny, but you get my drift."

Patrick stared at her, and then at Max, speechless. He was exhausted. He could feel his muscles quivering under his skin. His side ached where he had fallen. The wind cut through his clothes and chilled him to the bone. Ruby was right. He was helpless. And useless. There was nothing he could do to help here. Nothing at all.

"We'll see about that," retorted Boopie Cupid. "You might just be surprised, Ruby. There's more to Patrick than meets the eye."

The old Barrier-comber grunted. "Well, good luck to him, then." She reached out a rough hand and touched Patrick's cheek. She cleared her throat. "I'll be off, then," she said gruffly. "And I'd advise you to make tracks as well. It's not safe out here—not for you, and especially not for him."

Max roused himself. "I know. You're right," he said. He moved to Patrick's side and put his arm around him. "Walk between Boopie and me, Patrick. Then you'll be less noticeable. Ready? Come on."

"Bye, Ruby. Thanks," said Boopie.

With a wave the old woman turned away. Max, Patrick, and Boopie went on up the hill.

Patrick found his voice. "Boopie . . . Max . . . what's happening? Why couldn't I get through to you on the computer? What's happening here? I don't understand!"

Max frowned, his eyes on the ground. "This business," he said, jerking his head back toward the Barrier, "started a week ago—the day you brought Estelle home. I didn't hear a thing about it; I was busy at the studio working on the computer—and Lucky Lamont. The power fused as you came through—well, of course you know that. I've had quite a few problems with the computer ever since. And Lucky's had to have completely new circuits."

"Will he be okay?" asked Patrick. He still remembered the horror he'd felt as Lucky Lamont, the "Finders Keepers" host, had gone mad before his eyes. Of course, he hadn't known then that Lucky was a robot.

"Oh, he'll be all right," shrugged Max. "He's the least of our worries."

They reached the top of the hill and started walking quickly down the road that led to the TV studio, leaning forward into the wind. Patrick looked around. Everything seemed so *ordinary*. It would be easy for him to think he was in some street at home. But this thought had barely crossed his mind when there was a distant crack, like lightning, and a low threatening rumble that went on and on. The ground under their feet began to shudder. Max, Patrick, and Boopie stopped and clung together while the wind raged about them. Patrick shook his head. No, there was nothing ordinary about this place.

The trembling of the earth slowly subsided, and silently they started off again. But this time, they were half running. This was not a good place to linger.

"Anyhow," Max went on, "no one paid much attention at first. Even by Monday, when the girls got the computer through to you, there was no particular fuss being made. Well, that's obvious—we never even thought to mention it to you, did we? Just a few more Barrier breaks than usual—so what? It had happened before. But then . . ."

"It went on," Boopie broke in. "Tuesday, Wednesday . . . and getting worse every day. Break after break after break. And all in this one area. We tried to contact you, but first you weren't answering, and then the computer wouldn't link with yours at all. On the news they said it was just something that happens every hundred years or so. They're still saying that. But the Barrier-combers don't believe it, and neither do we. And I don't think even the experts do anymore, really. Yesterday they declared this a disaster area and sent the Agents in. They're in charge now—of the Barrier and the Guards, and of us. They're in charge of everything. And then today the ground started to shake. And this awful wind blew up . . ." She fell silent.

The studio was in sight now, but Patrick couldn't see the doorway. It was hidden by a moving mass of people, some of them carrying roughly painted signs.

"Oh, Max, there are more of them!" Boopie slowed to a walk. She pulled at the hood of her coat, covering as much of her face as she could. Patrick could see that she was trembling.

"Who . . . who are they?" he stammered.

"Barrier-combers," said Max. "Keep your voice down. We'll have to take this very slowly and quietly." Patrick glanced at him. His voice was steady, but his face was grim. "Patrick, stay between us and keep your head down, like Boopie. We don't want to stir them up."

They walked toward the crowd.

"Who've we got here?" someone called. "Oh, dear, some Channel 8 bods trying to get to work, is it?"

"Don't answer. Keep walking, sweetie pie," Boopie said.

Patrick did as he was told, although his legs felt like jelly. He kept his eyes down and let the others lead him through the maze of bodies that blocked their path.

"Don't say much, do they?" croaked a voice behind them. "Think they're too good for us, because they work for a TV station, I suppose." The crowd murmured, but no one touched the three friends. They moved on, a few steps at a time.

"Your bosses should be ashamed!" someone shouted. "Taking the food out of our mouths! And for what? A game! Ban the Finders!"

"Ban the Finders! Ban the Finders!" chanted the crowd, pressing in around them.

Patrick risked a quick look ahead and his heart leaped. The door was just in front of them now. Boopie and Max guided him toward it.

"Ban the Finders! Ban the Finders!" shouted the Barrier-combers.

Boopie pulled a card out of her coat pocket and slipped it into a slot on the door. It clicked, and she pulled the door open a crack.

"In!" she breathed to Patrick, and pushed him through. As she did, her hood was caught by the wind and blew back, showing her blonde curls. She grabbed at it in panic, but it was too late. There was a second's shocked silence, then . . .

"It's her!" someone roared. "It's her! Boopie Cupid! Get her!"

7

Fast Forward

The crowd surged forward. Boopie and Max flung themselves through the door and slammed it, just in time.

Inside they leaned against the wall, panting. Muffled shouts of rage and the sounds of angry fists and feet thudding against metal reached their ears.

"My fans!" joked Boopie weakly.

"Stupid fools!" raged Max. "As if it's your fault!"

"They blame Boopie?" said Patrick slowly. "For what's happening to the Barrier? For the fence, and the Agents, and everything?"

"Oh, yes," said Max. "But not just Boopie—everyone connected with 'Finders Keepers.' It's just Boopie they recognize, because they've seen her on TV. If they'd known I was in charge of the computer it would've been me they'd have gone for. I'm the real villain, as far as they're concerned."

"He's a ma-ad scientist," sang Boopie in a spooky voice. She waggled her fingers at Max, then gave a laugh that was more like a sob. "He's been destroying the Barrier for years by bringing Finders here from the other side, you know, Patrick! Everyone's saying so, so it must be true, right?"

"Shut up, Boopie," Max said. "Don't even joke about it. They really believe it."

"I know," said Boopie quietly. "And the trouble is, they're not the only ones anymore."

There was a final ringing thud on the door, and then silence. The Barrier-combers had given up.

"Thank goodness!" Boopie groaned. She pulled out a packet of chewing gum and put two pieces in her mouth. "Anyone for gum?" she asked, trying to smile.

"No thanks!" frowned Max. "Vile stuff! And don't let me find it around the computer, either, Boopie."

Boopie rubbed at her face, leaving grimy smears on her cheeks. She looked at him, reproachfully.

"You're right. Sorry I spoke," said Max, though she hadn't said a word. "Okay. Let's get to the computer room. Now Patrick's here we might have a chance of getting somewhere."

Patrick took a deep breath. "Max," he said, as firmly as he could. "What can I possibly do to help?"

Max looked at him patiently. "You're going to tell us what's wrong, so we can try to fix it, of course."

"Me! How would I know what's wrong?"

Max scratched his head with exaggerated patience. "Let's face it, Patrick, the problem isn't on our side of the Barrier."

"Isn't it?" Patrick stared at him.

"Of *course* it isn't. That's obvious! Did you bump your head when you landed or something?

Now—what's the story? What's happening on your side?"

"N-nothing," Patrick stammered, feeling completely useless.

"Nothing! But that's impossible!" Max looked confused. Boopie tried to say something, but he waved her away. He stared hard at Patrick. "Now," he said, very slowly and clearly. "This is very important. Think sensibly, Patrick, before you speak. You're telling me that everything's all as usual over there? That the clock is running normally?"

"The clock?" Patrick looked wildly at them both. What did a clock have to do with anything? Then a thought occurred to him. "The . . . um . . . the Chestnut Tree Village clock's running a bit fast," he said. "Is that what you mean? It's funny . . . it doesn't usually—"

"Running fast? How fast?" barked Max, his eyes glittering.

"Oh, I don't know," said Patrick. "Not much. Five minutes or so—"

"*Five minutes!*" Max tore at his hair, almost jumping up and down on the spot. "Five minutes!" He advanced on Patrick. "Why didn't you say so before? How can you calmly stand there and tell me—"

"Max, Max!" Boopie darted forward and put her arm around Patrick. "You're scaring him. Calm down! You've forgotten. Patrick doesn't know about the clock. He doesn't know, Max. None of them do, over there. Remember?"

Max deflated like a punctured rubber toy. He slapped his hand to his forehead and shook his head. "Stupid," he mumbled. "Sorry, Patrick. I'm overtired. I did forget. Mind you, I can't understand how your people haven't . . ." He looked up. "Listen—this is really serious. Even worse than I thought. If only we'd been able to contact you earlier! We've got to get you back. You've got to get that clock fixed. Right now. Or we're all in deep trouble. Come on!" He grabbed Patrick and Boopie's arms and began to run, dragging them, protesting, behind him.

"Max! Max!" gasped Patrick, plucking at Max's jacket as they thumped down the empty corridors past dozens of identical pale green doors. "What's the matter? What's the clock got to do with it?"

"It's got everything to do with it," puffed Max, without turning around to look at him. "Clocks weaken the Barrier between our two time streams—you know that, don't you?"

Patrick nodded. "That's why there are Barrier breaks sometimes, right?"

"Right. Well, look, all clocks affect the Barrier a bit, especially big ones, and especially when they strike the hours. We've known that for hundreds of years over here. Every school kid learns it. But it's only been in the last few years, since we've been able to investigate your side using computers like mine, that we've discovered that over there there are certain clocks that have a particularly powerful effect. And that's because they're not ordinary clocks at all." Max slowed to a walk, breathing heavily. "Right. Here we are," he said, pointing.

The computer room door looked exactly the same as all the others that lined the corridor. Blank, unmarked, and painted pale green. If he'd been by himself Patrick could never have worked out which was the right one. Max threw open the door and hurried inside. Patrick and Boopie followed, and as Patrick looked around the small room he drew an excited breath.

It was just as he remembered it. Here he had met Max for the first time and seen the amazing "Finders Keepers" computer. Here Boopie had explained how the "Finders Keepers" game was played and watched Max send him back to his own time stream, to try to find one of the Seekers' missing objects and qualify to win a prize. He remembered how confused and scared he had been then. And how thrilled, when he had succeeded— not just once, but three times, in the end.

Boopie seemed to know what he was thinking. For a moment the worry left her face as she grinned at him. "Champion Finder returns to scene of triumph," she said.

Max turned to face them. "Now, be calm, everyone," he said, tugging at his hair and looking very wild around the eyes. "Patrick, listen. We haven't got much time." He stopped, then laughed bitterly. "That's truer than you know." He tugged at his hair again and made an effort to calm down. "As I said, we now know that on your side of the Barrier there are certain clocks that are much more important than the others. They're important because they keep time, for their area. We call them Sector Timekeepers. Now, if one of these starts to run fast—or slow, for that matter—"

"But *all* clocks keep time," interrupted Patrick, feeling stupid.

"No, no, no!" Max shook his head. "Pay attention, Patrick! The Sector Timekeepers aren't ordinary clocks. They don't just *tell* time, they *keep* time. Keep it steady, keep it regular. They're very, very accurate themselves, usually. But sometimes, just like ordinary clocks, they go a bit wrong."

Patrick stared at him.

"They *control* your time, sweetie," explained Boopie. "If they run even a little bit slow, time goes more slowly for you. If they run fast, time goes faster."

"Good heavens, boy," exclaimed Max, infuriated by Patrick's wide eyes and obvious bewilderment. "What's the matter with you? Don't you believe us? Haven't you *noticed* that some days go faster than others?"

Patrick stood motionless, while pieces of the strange jigsaw fell into place in his head. Long days that dragged, other days that flew by, for no apparent reason. This last week, which had passed so quickly. This morning, when time seemed to have gone into fast forward. The people at the shopping center, late, busy, rushing. And the Chestnut Tree Village clock running five minutes fast.

He looked at Max and licked his lips. "Our clock is one of those? Those Sector Timekeepers? Our time's going fast because *it's* going fast?"

"Yes!" shouted Max, pounding his fists together. "And that means . . . ?"

"And," said Patrick, working it out, "that means our time stream's going faster than yours. We're out of sync with each other. And so the Barrier, which is in between us, is getting sort of stretched. And that's why there are so many breaks."

"All right!" Max nodded violently. "You've got the picture. It happens quite often that we're a few seconds out of sync. It's a bit inconvenient, but it doesn't last. The clockmaker in charge of the Sector Timekeeper adjusts the clock so it's running accurately again. We know from the records that there has been the odd Barrier disaster, presumably because of something quite serious that took the clockmaker a while to fix. That's what the experts are saying is happening here.

"But they must be starting to realize by now that it's much more serious than it's ever been before. And they don't know what we know. If what you're saying is true, the clockmaker's not on the job at all! The clock's out of control. And now we're *minutes* out—*five minutes*, you say—oh, my aching head! And getting worse every second. The strain on the Barrier must be terrific! It's literally breaking itself to bits."

"Could something have *happened* to the clockmaker?" asked Boopie in a small voice.

"Almost certainly, I'd say," Max muttered. "I hadn't counted on that." He stood for a moment in silence, while the others watched him.

"What now?" Boopie said.

Max stared past Patrick at the computer. His eyes darkened. "We've got to fix the clock ourselves. Slow Patrick's side down. Before the whole thing goes up."

Patrick swallowed and stared at Max, not knowing what to say. His head was full of questions that he couldn't put into words. His stomach felt fluttery. He jumped as a light tap sounded on the door.

"Max," called a voice. "Max, Boopie, are you in there? Let me in! It's Estelle!"

8

"This Isn't a Game!"

Patrick watched as Boopie opened the door and Estelle slipped inside. "Did you make contact?" he heard her ask as she came into the room. "What did Patrick say?"

Boopie whispered something in her sister's ear and she spun around, her eyes wide. She saw Patrick smiling shyly beside Max. "Oh, no!" she cried. "Oh, Patrick, dear heart, why are you here? You shouldn't be here! Max!" She faced Max angrily. "How could you do this? How could you! It's so dangerous for Patrick, and for you. The Agents told you not to use the computer anymore. They *ordered* you not to! If they find out . . ."

"They won't find out, Estelle," said Max coolly. He looked down his nose at her. "There was too much interference to talk through the TV set. Patrick couldn't hear me. I had to get him over here so he could fill me in. I had no choice."

"No choice? No choice? Oh, what rubbish," raged Estelle, her eyes flashing. "It's bad enough putting yourself at risk. But how could you get the *child* involved!" Patrick was fascinated. When Estelle had been his family's baby-sitter she'd never ever lost her temper. She wouldn't have said boo to a goose. Being back at home on this side of the Barrier certainly suited her.

Max raised his chin. "It is very far from rubbish, Estelle," he said in his most superior voice. "Patrick quite understands. Don't you, Patrick?" He looked sideways at Patrick, and despite his lofty manner Patrick could see that Estelle was making him feel rather nervous, even guilty.

"It's okay, Estelle," he said, crossing over to her. She took his hand, but went on frowning.

"You don't understand, dear heart," she said. "Things here are very bad. I came to warn Max and Boopie—I managed to get away from the canteen for a few minutes, but I'll have to get back soon, before they miss me. It's so busy in there. Barrier Guards and Agents, as well as the usual staff. There are Agents everywhere, Max. And everyone's talking about 'Finders Keepers.' It's not just the Barrier-combers anymore. Now everyone's saying it. They're saying it's not a natural disaster. They're saying that 'Finders Keepers' caused the whole thing. That the computer moving Finders to and fro across the Barrier has damaged it beyond repair."

"The idiots!" Max almost spat the words.

"But they're almost right, aren't they?" said Estelle quietly. "That's why you're so worried, isn't it, Max? I was thinking about it on my way here. All this trouble has only happened since Patrick used the computer to bring me back home from his side. It was *me* coming back that mucked everything up, wasn't it? The shock to the Barrier has affected the Sector Timekeeper. This whole thing is *my* fault, isn't it?"

She faced Max defiantly, her fists clenched. He wouldn't look at her. "That's what you think, isn't it, Max?" she went on. "Go on, admit it!"

"Estelle, *I* brought you back," whispered Patrick. "You didn't even know what was happening. So, if that's what it is, really, then it's *my* fault."

"No, it isn't, Patrick! *I* sent Estelle over to your side by mistake in the first place," shrilled Boopie. "It's *my* fault."

"Well, it's my computer," said Max flatly. He rubbed his eyes with the back of his hand. "If it's anyone's fault, it's mine." He deliberately stood upright, straightening his hunched shoulders. "And I'm the one who has to put it right," he said. "Obviously the clockmaker's out of action. So there's only one thing to do. I'll have to go over to Patrick's side myself, find out what's wrong with the clock, and fix it."

"Yes!" Patrick was overjoyed. "That's right! Of course! You could go over like Estelle did, Max. You could fix the clock, and then I could show you our side, and our TV and computer shops and everything. That'd be great! And . . ." His voice trailed off as he noticed the expressions on his friends' faces. They looked stricken. "What's the matter?" he asked, confused.

Max was silent. "What's the matter?" Patrick demanded again. "What's wrong?"

"It's just . . ." Estelle hesitated, looked at Max and Boopie Cupid, bit her lip, and went on. "People from your side of the Barrier seem to be able to move through it backward and forward without causing any trouble, dear heart. We've been bringing Finders like you over here and sending them back for years. But it looks like people from our side are different. I got over to your side without any problems. But when I came *back*, well, you know what happened. The computer blew up, the Barrier started cracking up, the Sector Timekeeper went crazy."

Patrick stared. "So . . ." he began.

"So," Boopie said passionately, "so Max *can't* go over to your side, because he couldn't get *back*! If he tried to come back, the whole disaster would happen again."

Patrick shook his head in frustration. "But we don't *know* that, Boopie. It might have just been a freak accident, with Estelle. It might have been because there were two people coming back instead of one. It might . . . we don't *know* it, Max!" He turned to Max in appeal.

Max smiled at him and patted his shoulder. "Spoken like a scientist, Patrick," he said. "You're right. We don't know it. We only suspect it. But unfortunately the suspicion, at this point, is too strong to ignore. I couldn't risk this happening again." He stared at the computer. "No," he went on calmly, "if I cross over to your side I won't even try to come back. If I go, it's for good."

"You're not going!" cried Boopie. "Don't even think about it, Max."

Max shrugged. "I don't think I have a choice, Boopie. And think of what I'd see . . ." His lips curved, a light appeared in his eyes, and for a moment he looked very young.

"You wouldn't have long to enjoy it, Max," Estelle cut in. "You know you can't live on the other side. The Trans Barrier Effect will get to you. After a few months you'll feel your memory going. Then you start fading. Fading. You can feel it. I remember the feeling. It's not pleasant."

"Oh, Estelle!" pleaded Boopie. "Don't talk about it!"

Estelle ignored her and went on looking at Max, staring him down. "He's being all heroic. He's being stupid. I'm just reminding him of the plain facts," she said coldly.

"I know the facts, Estelle!" Max glared at her. "I know them better than you do! I know what I'd be letting myself in for. It's my business!"

"No, it's not!" retorted Estelle. "It's all our business! We love you. And we need you. You can't go!"

"Well, what am I supposed to do?" shouted Max. "Go on! What are we supposed to do? Let the clock run wild? Let Patrick's world go crazy? Let the Barrier tear itself to bits, and us with it?"

"No," said Estelle coolly. "We find another way. That's all. We just find another way."

"I'll do it!" The words had left Patrick's mouth before he had even thought about them properly. He watched as the others looked at him in silence. What did he mean? What could he do? He swallowed. "I mean," he said carefully, "that I'm the Finder. I'll find the clock-maker and get the clock fixed."

"Patrick," said Max, after a short silence, "I've never heard of a Sector Timekeeper clockmaker going missing before. They never stray far from their clocks. I think that whatever happened last Saturday at ten o'clock— the shock of it—must have affected the clockmaker as badly as it affected the clock. It's possible that he or she might not be able to help us anymore."

"You mean he might be *dead*?" Boopie breathed. Es-telle covered her face with her hands.

Max looked uncomfortable. "They're odd beings, the clockmakers," he said. "No one knows much about them. Except that the clocks are their lives. The clocks depend on them, and they depend on their clocks. If the shock to the clock was great enough . . ."

Patrick thought about the Chestnut Tree Village clock as he'd last seen it. It was running fast, yes. It was a bit scratched and battered, yes. But it wasn't finished yet. He shook his head. "I don't believe the clock-maker's dead," he said firmly. "And I'll find him. I will. Let me try, Max." He saw Max and Estelle exchange serious glances, and appealed to Boopie. "Tell them, Boopie! I can do it, can't I?"

A shadow of doubt flickered across Boopie's face, and then it was gone. She nodded fiercely. "Of course you can! You're our champion Finder, aren't you? Of course you can do it, sweetie pie." She turned to the others. "He has to try, you know," she said seriously.

"We don't have much time, Boopie," Max said. "And this isn't a game. If Patrick can't . . ." He looked at Patrick, and stopped.

If Patrick can't do it. That's what he was going to say, Patrick thought. If Patrick fails. If he can't find the clockmaker. If the clockmaker isn't there to be found. If the clock doesn't get fixed, then it's the end. For the Barrier—and for all of us. He shivered.

Suddenly Estelle stiffened in alarm. "Listen!" she said. Patrick looked at her in surprise, and then he heard it, too. The sound of thudding feet, quite a few of them, outside in the corridor. Muffled now, but getting louder. Getting closer. Boopie gave a small shriek.

"It's them!" Estelle's eyes were dark with fear. "The Agents! Max, we've got to get Patrick out of here! If they find out you've been using the computer after all this— if they find Patrick, they'll—"

Max looked quickly around the small room. There was nowhere to hide. He spun to face Patrick. "All right!" he rasped. "All right. Go for it, son. See what you can do for us." He pulled Patrick into position, ran to the computer, and started punching keys. "Stand absolutely still," he ordered.

The tramping feet thundered to a halt outside. A fist beat on the pale green door. "Open up!" ordered a harsh voice.

"How . . . how will I tell you if I can't find the clockmaker?" Patrick could hardly get the words out. "How much time have I got?"

"Open up in there!" The fist beat on the door again.

"Max, hurry!" urged Estelle under her breath. "I don't think the lock's going to hold." She jerked her head at Boopie Cupid, and they ran on tiptoe to the shuddering door. They bent forward together, leaning against it with all their strength.

"I'll have to leave the channel open," gabbled Max, intent on what he was doing. "Then you can call through the TV in the usual way, anytime you like. Just don't stand directly in front of it. We don't want you over here again. As for time . . ." His brow wrinkled. "Nothing's normal. The usual rules might well not apply. For one thing, I don't think time will stand still anymore while you're across the Barrier. You've got—I don't know, Patrick! Depends on how fast the clock's running now. All I know is, if it gets to the big one— the twelve o'clock strike—without being corrected, we're history. Eleven will be bad enough. If I haven't heard from you by eleven o'clock our time, I'll come through myself. Now! Get ready! I've got the fix!"

"What's going on in there?" the voice outside demanded. The door rattled and shook. Boopie and Estelle looked back over their shoulders at Patrick, their faces strained and pale.

"Patrick, take care," whispered Estelle. "Take care!"

Patrick felt his eyes prickle. "Will you be all right?" he asked.

"We'll be okay. Don't worry about us," chirped Boopie, nodding encouragingly at him. "Good luck! Good finding!"

"Go, boy, go!" grunted Max.

Patrick plunged into darkness.

9

The Split

Round about the time the Agents started beating on Max's door, Claire was prowling along the paperback racks of the Chestnut Tree Village bookshop, tilting her head to one side to read the titles. Danny was tugging at the back of her T-shirt. "Claire, I'm thirsty," he complained. She frowned and ignored him. "Claire?" he repeated. "I'm thirsty. I want a drink."

"Danny, go back outside the shop and watch for Patrick like I told you," ordered Claire, moving on down the shelves. "Boy, will he get it when I tell Dad he went off like that. He was supposed to stay close and do what I said."

"But Claire . . ."

Claire turned around, put her hands on her hips, and glared down at him. "Now look, Danny, I've got to get this book. That's what I came to the shops for. We did what you wanted and watched the clock."

"But it didn't strike ten twice!" protested Danny.

"Danny, I *told* you—oh, never mind!" sighed Claire. "Look, as soon as Patrick comes we'll go and get a drink, okay? Then I've got to go to the lost property office. But that means I've got to get the book *now*. So you go and

watch for Patrick. He'll come back to the clock any minute and he won't be able to find us. Then he'll wander off and get lost. Then we'll never get our drink, will we? Go on, be a good boy!"

"Okay, okay," grumbled Danny. He wandered out of the shop and looked over at the clock, through crowds of bustling people. Patrick wasn't there. He heaved a loud sigh and pushed his nose onto the cool glass of the shop window. Through it he could see Claire, again walking along the shelves, her head on one side, reading the book titles. He kicked his toe against the smooth tiles on the floor. He was bored and thirsty. This had all been pretty disappointing so far. He pulled his golf ball out of his pocket and wrapped his fingers around it. He liked the way it just fitted into the palm of his hand. He liked its smooth, round, hard feeling.

He checked the clock again. Still no sign of Patrick. He looked back into the shop. Claire was reading the back of one of the books now. She didn't look up.

Danny came to a decision. It was time to take matters into his own hands. At this rate it would be time to go home before he got his drink, or had a go at "Finders Keepers" and won his prize, or anything. For sure Patrick had gone into that big store near the clock, with all the radios and TVs and things in it. It was just across the plaza. All right. Danny would just go over to the door and look in. And if he saw Patrick, he could call him. Then they'd come back for Claire, and *then* they could have a drink.

He pushed himself away from the shop window and

looked back at Claire. She was still reading. Danny began trotting cautiously over the smooth floor of the plaza. He passed the clock. It was ticking very loudly today, he thought. He fingered his golf ball nervously, expecting any minute to hear Claire's angry voice calling him back to the bookshop.

But no voice came, and quite quickly he was at the department store door. He peered inside. The lights were bright, and there were lots of people walking around looking at things. Patrick wasn't there—not near the door, anyway. Danny edged inside. He knew he shouldn't go far. This was the sort of big shop where kids got lost. All the aisles looked the same.

He craned his neck to look down to the end of a row of TV sets. Patrick liked TV. Maybe he was there. But the TV screens flickered silently in their line. No one was there to watch them. The aisle was empty.

Danny sighed, and then he gasped. And blinked. Once, twice. The aisle was empty. Then—suddenly— it wasn't. Someone had just . . . *appeared* from nowhere, in front of the last TV set in the row. And the someone was . . .

"Patrick!" Danny squeaked, his eyes popping. "Patrick!"

Outside the bookshop Claire was scanning the plaza with a worried frown. Where on earth was Danny? Where was he? She'd told him to stay right here. She'd seen him through the window only a few minutes ago. She stuffed the book she had bought into her shoulder bag. What if he'd been kidnapped by some loony? What if, right now, some stranger was hustling him away, out of the shopping center, where they'd never find him? Her cheeks and forehead grew hot. Mum—what could she say to Mum?

Back in the department store, Danny was darting forward. "Patrick!" he shrieked. "Where were you? Where did you come from?" He stared wide-eyed as his brother stumbled toward him, past the flickering TV screens. Patrick was shaking his head as if he'd just woken up. He stared vaguely at Danny and didn't answer.

"Was it a magic trick, Patrick? Was it?" demanded Danny.

Patrick licked his lips. "'Finders Keepers,'" he murmured. "I've got to . . ." His voice trailed off.

"Wow!" squealed Danny in excitement. "'Finders Keepers'! Did you get any prizes, Patrick?"

"Prizes?" Patrick shook his head again. Then he took a deep breath and rubbed roughly at his eyes. When he took his hands away he looked more awake. But then he frowned. "Danny, what are you doing here?" he said. "Where's Claire?"

"Over there." Danny stabbed a chubby finger back over his shoulder.

"Well, look, you tell her I've got to do something, and I'll see her at the clock at eleven. Okay?" Patrick brushed past Danny and made for the door of the store.

"But Patrick—" Danny jiggled up and down in frustration. The golf ball fell from his hand and he crouched to pick it up.

"Just tell her, Dan," Patrick called. "It's important. I'll explain later. Promise!" He waved in Danny's general direction and was gone. Danny knelt where he was for a minute. Then he slowly stood up and, with a small, mischievous smile, began to edge down the aisle, toward the last TV set in the row.

Claire pulled her arms across her chest and hugged herself tightly, her eyes darting around the plaza. Stupid! She was being stupid. Obviously Danny had gone off looking for Patrick, or found him, or something. Or maybe he was in front of the clock, where she couldn't see him.

She walked rapidly to the center of the plaza and right around the clock. It ticked on, fast and loudly. As she moved toward the front again it struck the half hour. Half-past ten? It couldn't be! She checked her own watch and shook her head. She must have been in the bookshop much longer than she'd thought. Even her watch showed twenty-five minutes past ten. The time had flown. She looked curiously at the clock. The crack on the blacksmith's arm was really obvious, as were the missing chips of paint on the tree. The clock had been damaged. You'd think someone would fix it. She remembered the little china bird in her shoulder bag. She'd been going to hand it in. After Patrick came back. After they'd had their drink. Danny had been thirsty. Danny . . .

"Danny, where are you?" she whispered. Then she stiffened. Patrick had emerged from the department store across the plaza and was running toward her.

"Patrick!" she called, for once oblivious of the stares of passersby. She ran to meet him and grabbed his arm. "Patrick, have you seen Danny?"

Patrick tore himself free. "He's back there," he said quickly, jerking his head in the direction of the department store. "Near the TV sets. I've got to go! See you!"

"What? Where?" shouted Claire as he darted off again. "Patrick, wait! Where'll you be?"

"Clock. Eleven. Danny—ask Danny!" Patrick shouted back. She saw him hurtle to the clock, come to a skidding stop against the little white fence, and then begin slowly pacing around it.

Claire clicked her tongue in irritation. Little brothers were the pits! This was the last time she'd ever, *ever* take them anywhere. Look at that screwball Patrick! What did he think he was playing at? She flicked back her hair and started marching toward the department store door. Now that she knew Danny was safe, she was free to be furious with him. Disobedient little rat!

She stormed in through the store doors. Near the TV sets, Patrick had said. Oh, yes, that'd be right! She peered down the aisle lined with sets. On the screens people and cartoon characters mouthed silently, talking to no one. And at the far end, small and intent, golf ball in hand as usual, stood Danny.

Claire began to walk toward him. The little boy was so absorbed in what he was watching that he didn't even notice her. Good! She'd give him a shock he'd never forget. She crept forward, half smiling, imagining the shocked, guilty look on his face when she shouted. Soon she was only a few paces away from him, and he still hadn't looked away from the set. What was he watching that was so interesting? It could be anything. You never could tell with Danny. She leaned forward until she could see the screen, and frowned in confusion. There was nothing on it but a very fuzzy, jumpy picture of a small room. Nothing going on. Nothing happening. How odd!

She crept a little closer, then froze. Danny was moving. He was walking cautiously up to the TV screen. His lips were opening. What game was he playing?

"Let me in," she heard him say. A shiver ran up her spine. What . . . ?

"Let me in!" Danny repeated, more confidently. He stared straight at the TV screen and stretched out a hand. "I want to play, too! Let me play!" His whole body went rigid. The golf ball fell from his fingers.

And then he disappeared.

Claire screamed, blinked, screamed again. She clapped her hand over her mouth and stared wildly at the TV screen. She stepped forward and something rolled against her foot. Slowly she bent her head to look down. Danny's golf ball lay where he had dropped it. She stared at it, her throat aching. She looked again at the screen.

"Danny!" she whispered. "Come back!" But the screen flickered, unchanging. He was gone. Little

Danny. Gone. He'd be so frightened. She couldn't bear it. She had to do something. She had to help him. Her head felt as though it was going to burst. She took another step forward, till the screen was all she could see. "Danny!" she called. She heard her own voice as if it was echoing from very far away. "Wait! I'm coming!" She put out her hand as she had seen Danny do. "Let me in!" she pleaded. "I have to get in!" And shut her eyes as blackness closed in on her.

10

THE TIMEKEEPER

Patrick bent double over the white fence behind the clock, squinting at a little brass plate fixed to the back of the wooden chestnut tree. The sharp tops of the fence pickets pressed uncomfortably into his chest as he made out the words. "Donated and maintained by the maker, A. V. Varga," he read. His heart thudded.

A. V. Varga. To his surprise, the unusual name was ringing a bell in his mind. He'd seen it before somewhere. He straightened up, absent-mindedly rubbing his chest and thinking hard. Then suddenly, like a flash of light, he remembered. The antique shop, just across the plaza. The words, painted in gold on the window: "A. V. Varga, Proprietor." He hadn't paid any real attention to them at the time, of course. He'd had other things on his mind. But his memory had recorded them anyway, and now out they popped, just when he needed them.

So A. V. Varga, the maker of the Chestnut Tree Village clock, also owned the Chestnut Tree Village antique shop. What a stroke of luck! But then, of course, in another way it was just what you'd expect. Max had said the Sector Timekeeper clockmakers liked to keep close to their clocks. That would be hard to do in a shopping center—unless you owned a shop nearby. "Yes!" Patrick whispered triumphantly. He'd made a flying start. He'd discovered the identity of the clockmaker in a bare few minutes. Now—he crossed his fingers—now to find the clockmaker himself—alive and in one piece.

He marched confidently over to the antique shop, feeling elated and full of energy. As he went in, he saw with relief that there were no other customers. Just the young shop assistant he had met once before, hovering like a pale, fluttering shadow amidst the richly glowing china, silver, and glass, the fancy statues and old clocks ticking.

"Can I help you?" the young man said, moving forward to meet him.

"Could I speak to—um—the owner, please?" Patrick muttered. He looked nervously at the precious objects clustered around him, hunched his shoulders and wiped his damp hands against the sides of his jeans. Suddenly he felt grubby and clumsy and young instead of confident and heroic.

The young man's face took on a regretful expression. "I'm so sorry," he said. "Miss Varga isn't here. She's not at all well, as a matter of fact. Not at all well."

Patrick's stomach flipped sickeningly. "Miss Varga? A. V. Varga? The owner of the shop? The clockmaker?" he persisted, to make sure.

The man nodded, eyeing him curiously.

Patrick found himself clasping his hands tightly

together. He forced himself to relax. "What's wrong with her?" he asked. He heard his own voice trembling.

The man's face changed from curiosity to concern. "Oh, I'm sorry. Are you a friend of Anna's? I didn't realize. Well, I'm afraid it's her heart. Last Saturday she took a very bad turn."

"When—when the clock, the big clock, struck ten twice?" Patrick had to know.

The young man looked surprised. "Well yes, as a matter of fact. It was a strange coincidence," he said. "The clock, of course, really is her life's work. Yes, well, Miss Varga was here at the time—actually in her apartment behind the shop—and I heard her call out. The clocks in the shop were chiming the hour, too, you see, and at first I didn't hear her, unfortunately. By the time I did, she was in a very bad way. And I remember the clock in the plaza was still striking. A second set of ten. Very strange." He thought about that for a minute, shaking his head.

"Where is she now?" Patrick urged. The clocks in the shop were ticking, ticking away the seconds, like the big clock in the plaza. He had to find Anna Varga.

"She's out of intensive care now, so they sent her back to the community hospital just across the road," the young man answered. He looked down at his hands. "But—ah—they say she's not likely to get better, you know. And she's not really *with* us, if you know what I mean. They're trying to trace her relatives. It's sad, though. They can't find anyone at all. She seems to have been absolutely alone in the world." He raised his eyes to Patrick and went on gently, "I think we have to accept that it's just a matter of time. After all, she's had a marvelous inning, hasn't she? Heavens, no one knows how old she is. She seems to have lived in the district forever. And she seems never to have had a day's illness in her life. No health records whatever, apparently."

Patrick stared at him. "Can *you* fix the clock?" he demanded abruptly.

The man looked confused. "Well, no, of course not," he said. "And anyway, no one touches that clock but Miss Varga. No one else would dare to. No one else has the authority." Then his brow wrinkled and his expression became suspicious. "Listen, are you *sure* you're a friend of hers?"

But Patrick had heard enough. He knew what he had to do. "Thanks!" he said hastily, and backed out of the shop. He turned toward the escalators and started running.

11

RESCUE

Claire struggled to her knees in the rough grass, only to be sent sprawling again by a wild gust of wind. She lay still for a moment, head spinning, eyes and ears straining. Where was she? What had happened? Something hard—the wall of a building, she thought—pressed against her back. The sky above her was dark and threatening. Shouts and whistles rose above the roaring of the wind. Then her mind cleared and she remembered. Danny! She had to find Danny! She pushed herself from the ground again and this time she managed to stay up. She crouched in the grass, her hair flying back over her shoulders, and forced her watering eyes to focus.

She was huddled against the back wall of a little red hut halfway down a hill in some sort of field, or that's what it looked like. The field—all of it that she could see, anyway—was surrounded by a high wire fence, against which crowds of shouting people were pressing. They looked as if they wanted to get in. Men and women in black uniforms—police, or soldiers,

maybe—were patrolling the inside of the fence, sometimes threatening the crowd with wicked-looking black
sticks.

Claire shook her head. None of this mattered. What
mattered was Danny. She had to concentrate. She
looked to her right and left. More people in uniforms—
mostly red uniforms this time. They seemed frantically
busy, staggering here, there and everywhere, shouting to each other. But there was no little figure in
bright blue T-shirt and baggy shorts to be seen. No
Danny.

Claire gripped the clumps of grass under her hands
and began to crawl away from the shelter of the red hut.
It blocked her view. Danny might be farther down the
hill, where she couldn't see him. She reached the corner and pushed herself into the open. The force of the
wind nearly bowled her over again, but she was ready
for it this time and braced herself against it. She looked
down the hill and her mouth fell open.

Behind a screen of black scaffolding a shimmering
wall rose up before her. A wall that seemed to have no
beginning and no end. But it had been damaged. Badly
damaged. Its shining surface was ripped and torn, and
all sorts of things—clothes, books, bowls, tins, lids,
toys, and a hundred other things—were bursting
through from the other side and tumbling to the
ground. Figures in overalls and yellow crash helmets
were swarming over the scaffolding, and hundreds of the
red-coated people clustered at its foot, dodging the fall-

ing objects and trying to push them back through the wall.

Claire, huddled on her hands and knees in the long grass, stared hypnotized at the weird scene before her. She couldn't move or think. She didn't know where she was. She didn't know what she was going to do. And Danny was nowhere to be seen.

"Oh!" The shriek burst from her as something hit her hard in the side. She tumbled over and someone fell with her, rolling her over, pressing her down, smothering her. She struggled violently to free herself, pushing and shoving at her attacker.

"Oi, take it easy!" Warm, plump hands grabbed her own and held them. Claire opened her eyes, her heart beating violently. This didn't sound like an enemy. She looked up into the pleasant, worried face of a young woman with a mop of curly red hair. Claire opened her mouth, but no words came.

"You okay?" asked the young woman. "Sorry, I didn't see you there. Tripped straight over you." Her forehead wrinkled as Claire struggled to sit up. "You okay?" she asked again. "You're awfully pale. Better just lie there for a minute." Her fingers found the inside of Claire's wrist and pressed down on it. Claire realized she was taking her pulse. She licked her lips.

"I'm all right," she managed to croak. "I'm fine. I just got a shock. I . . ." To her horror she felt her eyes fill with tears.

The young woman's forehead wrinkled even more.

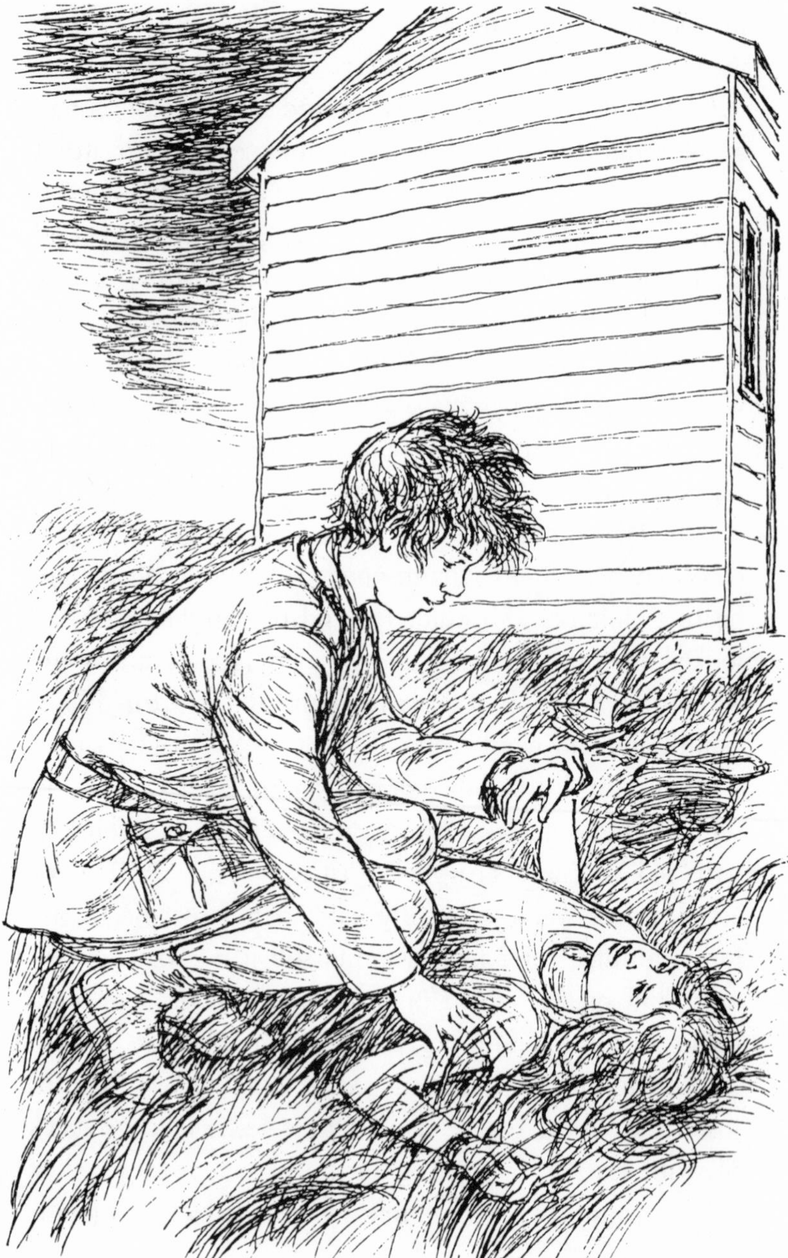

"Hey, don't cry!" she said, looking away and rubbing at her freckled nose roughly, in embarrassment. "Nothing to cry about. You shouldn't be inside the fence, you know that. How you *got* in I don't know. But I won't turn you in. Not this time, anyhow. If you promise on your honor you won't try to get in again." She stood up, staggering against the wind, and began brushing busily at her red jacket, as if it was the only thing she had on her mind.

Claire pulled herself together and sat up. She sniffed. The young woman stopped brushing and crouched beside her. She looked keenly at Claire. "Bit young to be a Barrier-comber, aren't you?" she asked casually. "And you don't look the best, kid. Pale as a ghost. What happened? Trouble at home? Run away, did you?"

Claire shook her head. "I—I'm looking for my brother. My little brother, Danny. He's lost here. He's all by himself. He's only four. I've got to find him."

The young woman looked shocked. "*Four!* How on earth? Look—we'd better report this." She scrambled to her feet and pulled Claire up beside her. "A kid like that could get into a lot of trouble in this place." As she spoke there was a rumble, like thunder. The ground trembled under their feet. Claire screamed. The young woman's eyes darted anxiously to the shining wall in front of them and the working red-and-yellow figures. "Better make it snappy," she said. "I've got to get back on duty. Look, first things first. I'll call from my box here and put out a warning to all the Guards, all right?

They'll be able to keep an eye out for the little kid—Danny, was it?"

Claire nodded. She felt exhausted. But at least something was happening. She was no longer alone.

"This yours?" The young woman pointed to Claire's shoulder bag, lying beside the red hut, its contents scattered in the grass.

"Oh, yes." Claire bent to retrieve her belongings, shoving them back into the bag. Comb, tissues, keys, wallet—and the book she'd bought from the Chestnut Tree Village bookshop. That book! How dearly she had paid for it. If only she'd let Danny stay with her. If only she'd waited and bought it later. If only . . . Her eyes filled with tears again.

Her new friend punched gently at her arm. "Hey, don't worry," she said. "We'll find him." She led Claire around to the front of the hut. "Come in out of the wind, and I'll call," she said. "Come on."

The hut was shaped like a sentry box, with a sharply sloping roof and tiny windows on either side of the door. Claire followed the young woman inside and almost lost her balance as the walls closed around her, cutting off the fierce wind that had buffeted her for so long. And the silence! It was blissful! She let out a long breath and took note of her surroundings. She was standing in a neat little office, with a desk and a chair, a filing cabinet, a noticeboard, a potted plant, and a phone. Everything fitted together perfectly, like the furniture on a boat or a camper.

"Sit down, why don't you?" the red-headed woman

said kindly. "Take the weight off your feet while I make this call."

Claire sank gratefully into the desk chair. Her knees were weak. She gazed vaguely at the noticeboard. A neatly printed notice took pride of place in the center. It was headed BARRIER GUARDS—SECTOR 9—DUTY ROSTER Her eyes traveled over it, took in the other items pinned around it. There were dozens of them: reminder notes, programs, notices, and photographs. This little place was obviously a home away from home. She half smiled, looking at the photographs. A big old dog, an older couple in a swinging chair, some people at a beach, and at the end her new friend smiling nervously between a smarmy-looking man and a blond girl in a yellow dress, under a glittering sign. What did the sign say? She leaned forward to look more closely. FINDERS KEEPERS. What? She drew a sharp breath, and the young woman looked over at her, the phone in her hand.

"You okay?" she enquired.

Claire pointed at the photograph and swallowed. "'Finders Keepers,'" she said.

The woman grimaced self-consciously. "Oh, yes," she said, and turned back to the phone. She pushed impatiently at its buttons. "I can't get through," she complained. "Lines are jammed, I suppose. This could take awhile."

Claire's thoughts were racing. "Finders Keepers." Patrick's game show. The game Danny was so fascinated by. "That's where he must be! At 'Finders Keepers,'" she blurted out, still staring at the photograph.

The woman turned around again and shook her head sadly. "Oh, no, love. He couldn't be there. The show's been shut down."

"But it couldn't have. My brother was there," Claire persisted. She jumped up, nearly knocking over the chair. "We have to go and see."

Her friend's pleasant, freckled face grew concerned. "Sit down, love," she advised. "You're a bit confused. They wouldn't have a four-year-old for a Seeker. Come on, think about it."

"No, no!" Claire cried. "Not *that* brother. Not Danny. My other brother, Patrick. He *was* there. He won prizes. I saw them. And Danny wanted to . . ."

"*What!*" The young woman's jaw dropped, and she clapped the phone down. Her freckled cheeks blushed bright red. "Patrick!" She smacked her forehead with her open hand. "Oh, what an idiot I am!" she exclaimed. "Of course! No wonder you look like a faded-out ghost. You're from the other side! Well, paint me purple and put a clothespin on my nose! Danny! Yes, I remember, that *was* his little brother's name. He told us. And you're the sister. The big sister. You're Claire!"

12
The Finder

Things were moving too fast for Claire. "You know Patrick?" she whispered at last.

"Know him! Know him!" grinned the young woman. "I owe my job to him, that's all. I was a Seeker on the show. He was my Finder. And, boy, did he do his job! He saved my bacon. You just ask him if he didn't. Wendy Minelli's my name. You just ask him . . ." Then suddenly the color and excitement ebbed from her face and it grew serious. "But listen, how did this happen?" she said slowly. "How come you're here? And the little bloke? We've got big trouble in this Sector, you know. The Barrier's unstable. The Agents are as nervous as cats about the other side. You shouldn't be here. There'll be huge trouble if anyone finds out."

She spun around, pulled open a cupboard, and took out a red jacket like the one she herself was wearing. "Put this on," she ordered, holding it out to Claire. "Put it on quickly! Then if any of the Agents see you, they won't catch on. They'll think you're one of us."

Scared and confused, Claire did as she was told, pulling the jacket on over her T-shirt. It felt scratchy and stiff. She did up the shiny buttons with shaking fingers.

Wendy pursed her lips and looked her up and down. "You'll do, I guess," she pronounced finally. "As long as no one gets too close. Now . . ." She sat on the desk, clasped her hands, and leaned forward. "You'd better fill me in. What's been going on? Where's Patrick?"

Patrick was hurrying down the ramp that led out of Chestnut Tree Village. The ticking of the clock, loud, harsh, and fast, seemed to follow him as he ran. He was on the trail, but there was so little time. Twenty-five minutes till eleven o'clock. Twenty-five minutes to find the clockmaker, to fix the clock, to stop Max from having to throw his life away by crossing the Barrier, to stop the Barrier from breaking to bits. Twenty-five minutes. He wondered briefly what Claire and Danny were doing now. Happily having morning tea in a café, probably, without a care in the world. He'd promised to meet them at eleven. Eleven o'clock again! He wondered if he'd be able to keep his promise.

Hot and panting now, Patrick ran off the ramp and onto the footpath, swerving to avoid two boys on skateboards as he pounded toward the pedestrian crossing. Thank heavens he knew where the hospital was! Thank heavens it was so close! What on earth would he have done otherwise? He resisted the temptation to check his watch. No point in fretting. He was going as fast as he could.

He waited at the light in a fever of impatience, crossed the busy highway, and started running again, his chest tight, toward the high gates that had looked, from the other side of the road, so much closer than they really were. And then at last he had reached them, and entered, and was running down the long drive, through a corridor of giant trees, up the few steps to the hospital's main entrance. There he paused. He had to calm down. They wouldn't let him in if he seemed silly or wild.

He combed his hair with his fingers, wiped the sweat from his hot face, and brushed at his jeans. Then he pushed open the door and moved into the coolness of the hospital.

A nurse in a pale blue uniform sat writing at the reception desk. She had smooth hair, blue eyes, and very thin, high eyebrows. She looked up at him inquiringly, raising her eyebrows even higher and twisting her pen between her long fingers.

"I'm here to see Miss Varga," said Patrick firmly. "Miss Anna Varga. Please."

"Are you a relative, dear?" the nurse asked rather sharply, and tapped the pen on the desk.

"No. Um—I'm a friend," Patrick said. It wasn't quite true, but he had to say something.

The nurse lost interest. "Visiting hours on this floor begin at two-thirty, dear," she said. "You can come back then, all right?" She flashed a smile at the top of his head and went back to her writing.

Patrick stood his ground. "Please," he said loudly. "Please. I can't wait till two-thirty. Couldn't I see her now? Only for a minute."

The nurse looked up again, thin eyebrows raised.

"I'm sorry, dear," she said, not looking as if she was sorry at all. "You'll have to run along. Come back this afternoon." She waited for a moment. Patrick didn't move. "Off you go, then," she added impatiently.

There was nothing to do but obey. Patrick couldn't just run past the nurse and start searching from room to room. She'd have him caught and thrown out as quick as a flash. At the door Patrick turned to look over his shoulder. The nurse was watching him coldly, making sure he really left.

He pushed through the door and the warm air outside hit him like a wave. He wandered down the steps and sat down on the clipped green lawn under a tree. He looked at his watch. Twenty to eleven. Twenty minutes to go. He picked aimlessly at the grass beneath his hand. What on earth was he going to do now?

Back on the other side of the Barrier, Danny was wondering the same thing. If this was "Finders Keepers," it wasn't what he had imagined at all. The people who shouted and pushed around him were like the people in the shopping center, when he had gotten lost in the fruit shop queue. They were all much taller than him, they all looked angry, and none of them seemed to notice he was there. He couldn't see anything, in front of him or behind, because of the forest of legs. But he knew he was outside, of course, because of the gray, rumbling sky above and the trampled grass under his feet. He couldn't understand it.

Then an idea came to him. Maybe "Finders Keepers"

was played in a big tent, like a circus. Maybe all these people were waiting to get in. They were certainly trying to get into something farther down the hill. He could tell that from the things they were shouting.

He patted his pocket for the twentieth time, checking for his golf ball. But the pocket was flat and empty. He'd dropped the ball in the department store. His lip trembled. It had seemed such a clever idea, to come here. But now it didn't seem clever at all. He thought about Claire, back in the shopping center. She'd be looking for him. She wouldn't know where he was. He whimpered, and his thumb crept into his mouth.

There was a crack, like lightning. Danny jumped. The crowd shouted with one voice and began pushing forward. Trapped in the mass of people, Danny was pushed forward, too. For a minute he thought he was going to be squashed. He could hardly breathe! And then, with a clang and a thump, something in front of them broke, shrill whistles sounded, and the crowd surged ahead.

Danny was swept along with them down the hill, stumbling over the grass, only just keeping his feet. He nearly tripped over the wire fence lying twisted and flattened on the ground, but saved himself just in time. It flashed across his mind that the fence must have been what had broken so that the crowd could get through. But there was no time to think about why the fence was there, or where he was now being driven. All he could do was concentrate on staying upright. On not being trampled by the yelling, excited grown-ups behind him.

Then, suddenly, the movement stopped. The crowd scattered and people began bending down, picking things up from the ground and stuffing them in shoulder bags and pockets. Danny stood still, bewildered. Wind roared around him, tearing at his clothes and hair. Ahead of him, very close, was a shimmering wall that seemed to be covered in metal bars. A huge black crack showed in the wall, and things were falling out of the crack, and scattering all over the grass below. Was this "Finders Keepers"? Was this the game? Not a quiz show, but a sort of treasure hunt?

Danny looked at the ground. By his feet he saw a leather glove. And a pink hair clip in the shape of a bow. He picked them up and put them in his pocket. Claire might like the hair clip, he thought. And maybe he could find the other glove, for Mum. For a minute he felt quite pleased. He started searching for more things to collect.

And then he saw the soldiers. Soldiers in red uniforms, and in black uniforms, too. Suddenly they were everywhere, closing in on the crowd. They were rushing at people, pushing at them roughly, trying to drive them back. The black-uniformed soldiers had big sticks.

The back of Danny's neck prickled. Still the people bent to the ground, gathering things as fast as they could, backing away from the soldiers but never looking up. Danny stood frozen, clutching at his pocket. A group of people staggered backward toward him, a huge soldier in black yelling and waving his stick close behind them. They were going to run into him. He'd be crushed. Or, even worse, the soldier would get him. Danny stared, horrified, at the shining black stick as it thrashed the air. He had to move. He had to.

He tore his feet from the ground, tripped, and scrambled away on all fours. The hard earth and clumps of grass hurt his hands, but he kept going, scuttling like a mouse, panting and shaking, head tucked down, eyes shut, expecting every moment to feel a hard hand on his neck, the thump of a stick on his legs.

But it was his shoulder that was thumped as he cannoned straight into something hard. He gasped and opened his eyes. And then he saw that he had bumped into the corner of a house he hadn't noticed was there. A little red house, sitting by itself in the field. He looked back over his shoulder. The fight was still going on behind him. He crawled around to the back of the little house and curled himself into a ball against the wall. It was shadowy here, and he could stay out of the way.

Be hidden. Be safe, maybe. He lay as still as he could, shaking with fright.

In the grass in front of him a splash of color caught his eye. He stared at it for a moment and then cautiously reached out a hand. His fingers grasped something cool, hard, and round. Curious despite his fear, he pulled the object toward him. It was a bird. A small, blue-and-yellow china bird with a round body and tiny tail and wings. Its little beak was open, as if it was singing, and its painted eyes were perky and bright.

Danny gently touched the bird's beak with his cheek. His fingers curled protectively around its smooth, round chest. It felt friendly and familiar to him. It fitted into his hand just like his golf ball had, and it weighed about the same. It was very comforting.

"Stop!" shouted an angry voice close by. Danny's head jerked up, and to his horror he saw a group of people with bulging pockets and bags running straight for his shelter, pursued by a huge, black-uniformed figure waving a stick. He got to his feet, his find clutched in his hand.

The running people reached the hut and began weaving around it, jeering and laughing at the furious soldier.

"Hey, Wendy! You in there, Wendy?" shouted one, a white-haired old woman in a green cardigan, purple dress, and football socks. She rapped on the wall of the hut as she scooted around the corner. "Hey, Wendy! Don't think much of the help you've got in. Can't run for nuts! You ought to give him the sack!"

"Get back where you belong or you'll be sorry, you miserable lot," roared the soldier, spitting with fury. He banged on the wall of the hut himself. "Minelli!" he shouted. "Get out here. Now!"

Danny decided it was time to leave. He bent his head against the wind and began trotting up the hill toward the trodden-down fence. Behind him, above the sound of the wind and the rumbles of the sky, he could hear shouts and thuds. He lowered his head even farther and pushed on.

Back at the sentry box, Wendy Minelli had come outside and taken charge. "You've got what you came for, you lot," she was calling good-naturedly to the rebel group. "Fun's over. Just do what you're told now, will you? Do me a favor!" She singled out the ringleader— the old woman in the green cardigan. "Come on, now, Ruby. Do the right thing."

"Aw—okay." The old woman grinned delightedly. "But just for you, Wendy. Not for this idiot in the fancy hat." She dodged nimbly as the Agent swung at her with his stick. "Come on, you lot. Back to camp!" Waving and giggling, the ragged group turned and trailed back up the hill.

The black-uniformed Agent bared his teeth in rage and pulled at his peaked cap with its silver badge and shining brim. "Think they're so smart, don't they," he snarled. He turned on Wendy. "And I suppose you think you are, too, Minelli! Well, just let me tell you this! The kid gloves are off after today. That's the word. Tomorrow we'll be wiping the smiles off their cheeky faces. And about time!" He looked over Wendy's shoulder and he frowned. "Hey, you!" he barked. "What do you think you're doing?"

Wendy spun around to see Claire peeping from the door of the hut with startled eyes. "My partner," she said, as casually as she could. "We were on our tea break."

"Oh, how nice," sneered the Agent. "Well, tea break's over! Get back to the Barrier and do what you're paid for. Go on!"

Wendy hurried to Claire's side. "Come on," she muttered between clenched teeth. She half led, half pulled Claire out of the hut. Claire looked nervously over her shoulder. The Agent was still watching them suspiciously, tapping his stick against his boot. Beyond him, trudging up the hill, were the people Wendy had sent away. And wandering beyond them, higher up, she saw, with a shock, a small, very familiar figure.

"Danny!" she screamed. "Danny!" She struggled to break free of Wendy's firm grip. "Wendy, let go," she pleaded. "Let go. It's Danny! I've got to get to him!"

The watching Agent stiffened. "What are you playing at?" he roared. "Get a move on!"

"Keep walking," hissed Wendy, pulling Claire along. "Keep walking! You'll never make it past the Agent, Claire. If he takes you in for questioning, we're in deep trouble. We'll have to work till he loses interest in us. It's our only chance."

Tears streaming down her face, Claire stumbled on, away from Danny, toward the Barrier.

13

A Meeting

Patrick was prowling around the hospital building, looking for another way in. He knew there must be one. No building he'd ever seen had just one entrance. For a start, there'd be a fire escape, wouldn't there? He kept close to the shrubs that lined the path beside the building. Big old hydrangeas nodded their heavy blue heads as he brushed past them. They smelled of leaves and damp earth.

"Visiting hours start at two-thirty on this floor," the nurse had said. "Come back this afternoon." As he had sat on the grass, wondering what to do, he'd suddenly realized that without meaning to she'd given him an important piece of information. Anna Varga must be here—not upstairs, or in one of the back wings of the hospital, but somewhere here, in this old part. Or the nurse's order wouldn't have made sense.

Patrick stopped short. He could hear voices in front of him, around a bend in the path. He lowered his head and moved on as quietly as he could, sheltering against the hydrangeas. At the bend he stopped, edged forward, and peered out.

Two women in pink stood chatting on some narrow concrete steps that led from the path into the building. As Patrick watched, one of them flapped a duster on the stair rail. "Well, Elise, better get on with it, I suppose," she said. "I'm all behind this morning."

The other woman nodded. "I know," she agreed. "Honestly, I thought the clock was wrong when I looked earlier. Couldn't *believe* how the time had flown. Funny how some days are like that, isn't it?"

"Clocks!" laughed her friend, flapping her duster. "Don't talk to me about clocks, Elise. I heard enough about clocks in Number 12 this morning to last me all week. Clocks, clocks, clocks. And none of it making sense. And then she had the hide to call *me* a fool. *Then* she worked herself up till I thought she was having another heart attack. Gave me a terrible turn. You can do Number 12's lunch today."

The woman called Elise grinned. "I don't mind," she said. "Poor old duck. Sad, isn't it?"

"Yeah." The woman with the duster looked vacantly into the distance. "Sad." Then she roused herself and turned to go inside. "Still, it comes to us all, Elise, doesn't it?"

"S'pose it does," Elise agreed, and followed her inside.

Patrick crept along the steps and listened. The women's voices echoed faintly through the door. They were moving away. He climbed the steps, his hand wet and slippery on the smooth metal rail. He peeped inside. A long corridor lined with doors stretched away from him. Each door was numbered. At the far end he could see the two women, wheeling trolleys. They turned a corner and disappeared from view. Number 12, the first woman had said. In Room 12 there was someone who talked about clocks. Stuff that didn't make sense. He was sure he knew just who that was.

He began walking down the corridor. His shoes squeaked on the shining vinyl floor, and he tried to tiptoe. Rooms 6, 7, 8 . . . He resisted the impulse to check his watch. Just keep going, he told himself. Just keep going. Rooms 10, 11 . . . Room 12.

Patrick took a deep breath, opened the door, and slipped inside.

The room was dim. In a high bed by the window, propped up on three pillows, lay a tiny old woman with long white hair. She was so small and thin that her body hardly made a bump in the white bedclothes. Her eyes were closed, and her fragile, blue-veined hands rested on her chest.

Patrick tiptoed to the bed. "Miss Varga," he whispered.

The eyelids snapped open, and dark eyes met his. Patrick jumped. The eyes seemed to see straight through him. "Miss Varga, I'm Patrick Minter. I've come about the clock," he said.

She struggled to raise herself from the pillows. Her mouth opened. "My clock!" came the faint, cracked voice. "I've been telling them. No one listens. I have to get back to my clock. Tell them!" The black eyes were filled with fear.

"It's running fast, Miss Varga." Patrick forced himself to go on.

"No!" Anna Varga's head tossed on the white pillow. "No, it must not run fast," she groaned. "It must be accurate, to the second, do you hear me? I must go to it. Now!"

"Miss Varga, you're sick, and you can't go," said Patrick, looking back at the door. Her voice had risen. What if someone heard her and came in? "Tell me what to do."

But the old eyes had closed. When they opened again they were blank and dull. They focused on Patrick in puzzlement. "Who are you? What do you want?" droned the voice.

Patrick swallowed. "I . . . I'm Patrick. I've come about the clock, Miss Varga. Don't you remember? Your clock. In Chestnut Tree Village."

"Ah—yes—Chestnut Tree Village." Anna Varga's fingers plucked vaguely at the sheet covering her. "The shopping center. The big new road. Once there was a house there, before the road went through. A house and a farm and gardens. Once. And my clock. The Timekeeper." Her eyelids fluttered. Her voice droned on.

"Before, in the garden, there was a sundial. Before that, a rock. They were enough. The shadows marked the hours. The sun, and the shadow." Her voice dropped to a low murmur. Patrick had to strain to hear. "The old ways were best," said Anna Varga. "The sun never failed. But I was young. I didn't understand that then. I heard what others had done, in London, in

Switzerland, in France, in China, and I wanted to be like them. I wanted to make what they made, have what they had. So I made the clock. My wonderful clock. So long ago. So long . . ." Her hand moved to her throat. "So tired," she whispered. "So tired. Can't understand . . ." She closed her eyes.

Patrick chewed at his thumbnail. What should he do? He looked at his watch. It was ten to eleven! His stomach jumped sickeningly. He had to do something. He had to reach her, get her out of the dream world in which she was wandering. Now!

"The Timekeeper is running five minutes fast, Miss Varga," he said loudly and clearly.

"NO!" The old woman's scream sounded incredibly loud in the small room. Her eyes wide open now, fixed on Patrick, piercing him through.

"Tell me what to do, Miss Varga," Patrick pleaded. "Tell me!"

With an enormous effort the thin old hand moved to point at the bedside cupboard. "In there. My bag," said Anna Varga.

Patrick opened the cupboard door and pulled out an old black leather handbag. He held it up for her to see.

"Yes," she said. "Yes." For a moment her eyes closed, then they opened again. "The plans. Inside. Get them." She wet her lips with her tongue and again struggled to sit up higher on her pillows.

Patrick opened the bag. It was almost filled by a bulky folded paper. He lifted it out carefully and opened it flat on the cotton blanket. The paper was soft, thick, and yellowed with age. Its edges were furred and torn, and deep creases furrowed its surface, which was covered with a faint, spidery diagram.

Patrick squinted at the diagram in dismay. In the dim light he could make out little of it, and it was so complicated! Anna Varga's bony finger stabbed at the paper. "It must be the regulators," she muttered rapidly. "It can only be the regulators. All else is well, I know that. But to gain so much! I cannot understand it. Unless . . ." Her eyes widened.

She struggled on her pillows, pressed her hand to her heart and fell back. The plans slipped to the floor. Patrick exclaimed in horror and backed away from the bed.

"No!" gasped the old woman, as if reading his thoughts. "Get no one. They will not understand. They are fools here. They will delay you. And I will survive if the clock survives. Do you see? What you do for the clock you do for me. But you must hurry. Be strong! Take the plans. Go to the clock. You will find that one of the regulators has broken loose somehow. Replace it, and everything will be as it was. Do you understand?"

Patrick nodded. He picked up the plans.

"Go!" panted Anna Varga, clutching at her chest. "Go now, boy! Go!"

Patrick turned, and ran.

Down the corridor, out the door, down the stairs into the heat he pelted, the plans clutched in his hand. He rounded the corner of the building and pounded past the front entrance, where the unfriendly nurse in the blue uniform stood talking to a woman in a straw hat. The nurse looked shocked, then angry, and called out after him as he raced on up the tree-lined drive. Patrick didn't look back.

He checked his watch as he ran to the pedestrian crossing. Seven minutes till eleven o'clock. "Hold on, Max," he whispered. "Wait for me!"

At the crossing he had to stop. The lights were red, and several people were waiting to cross. Patrick hopped from one foot to the other. Then he had an idea. He could use this time. He unfolded the diagram and scanned it anxiously, trying to make sense of the fine lines and scratchy writing. It was clearer out here in the light. He picked out the outline of the tree, the sun behind it, the hole from which the squirrel peeped.

Then—"Regulator." The word leaped up at him from the old yellow paper. Once, then again. Several times. And each time it appeared, a line led from it to—a bird. A little drawing of a bird.

"What!" Patrick shouted the word aloud. The birds— the little birds that popped out of the tree on the hour. *They* were the regulators. And one *had* broken loose, just as Anna Varga had said. One had broken loose when the clock was shaken up last Saturday. It had broken loose and fallen into a flowerpot. It had lain there for a week, while Anna Varga lay helpless in a hospital and the clock ran faster and faster. And this morning it had been found. And now it was in Claire's shoulder bag. "Yay!" caroled Patrick, ignoring the nudges and grins of the kids standing around him.

The lights changed to green, and Patrick hurried across the road and raced for the shopping center entrance. From now on it was easy. All he had to do was get the bird from Claire and stick it back where it belonged. Easy!

"Easy! Easy!" he sang under his breath, running up the ramp. He felt wonderful. Nothing could go wrong now.

14

Disappearing Acts

On the other side of the Barrier, Danny dropped to the ground and crouched, exhausted and bewildered. Around him scattered groups of people talked and walked, huddling together for protection from the wind or comparing things they had found at the bottom of the hill. Below him a crowd had gathered to jeer at the black-uniformed soldiers who were mending the broken-down fence.

Danny slipped his thumb into his mouth and, with his other hand, held the little china bird to his cheek. He thought about Claire and Patrick, now certainly frantic with worry and phoning home. He thought about his mother and father. And for the first time he wondered if he'd ever see them again. Tears started dripping down his cheeks. He put down his bird and furiously wiped them away.

There was a loud crack and a long, low thundering sound from the bottom of the hill. Danny jumped to his feet in fright. Around him people began to scatter. The wind roared, the sky grew dark, and the ground began to tremble and shake. What was happening? Yelling men and women ran past him in panic, and then Danny was running, too, looking wildly around for a place to hide.

At Chestnut Tree Village the clock had begun striking eleven—six minutes early. And Patrick was running past it, making for the TV set in the department store, the clock plans clutched flapping in his hand. He glanced sideways as he ran. Where were Claire and Danny? He'd been so sure that they'd be waiting by the clock. It was running fast, but they knew that, and Danny loved to watch it strike. He couldn't think where they could be, but he knew he had no time to worry about it now. He had to get word to Max that all was well. That he'd found out what was wrong with the clock, and could get it fixed easily by the twelve o'clock strike.

He raced into the store, darted toward the TV aisle, and almost collided with a shop assistant patrolling the area. "Take it quietly, kid," grumbled the man. "And tell your friends the same, will you? This isn't a playground."

Patrick nodded rapidly and tried to sidestep him, but the man kept a hand on his shoulder, forcing him to wait. "Hear me, kid?" he demanded. "You know what I'm talking about. I've seen the three of you together. You tell them. The little tearaway *and* the girl, if you don't mind. She's old enough to know better. If I catch them playing hide-and-seek or sardines or whatever around these valuable sets again, there'll be trouble."

Patrick shook his head in confusion. "Are Claire and

Danny in *here?*" he asked. He heard the last clanging strokes of the clock die away. It was fast, he reminded himself, trying not to panic. Max wouldn't try to cross the Barrier till the real eleven o'clock. He had six minutes till then.

The man released him and shrugged disgustedly. "Not now. But half an hour ago they were, and you can tell them from me that disappearing acts won't get them out of trouble next time. All right?" He nodded severely, turned his back on Patrick and walked on, his hands behind his back.

Patrick waited until the man had moved some distance away, then slipped into the TV aisle. He padded to the end and stood to one side of the TV set, as Max had advised. He had to be careful. The line was open. It would be easy to cross over the Barrier without meaning to, if you stood in front. The TV screen stormed with snow. Max's computer room was just visible, like a wavy shadow on the screen, but it was empty. No sign of Max, or Boopie, or anyone at all. Patrick sighed. He'd have to wait.

He looked back up the aisle, to make sure the cranky shop assistant wasn't watching him. What had he meant, about Danny and Claire? Patrick wondered idly. Games of hide-and-seek around the TV sets? Disappearing acts? He couldn't imagine Claire getting involved with anything like that. He moved slightly, and something rolled against his foot. He looked down, puzzled, and saw Danny's golf ball. He picked it up and stared at it.

Disappearing acts . . . Oh, no! Patrick almost shouted the words aloud. For in a flash he'd remembered Danny's face staring at him in wonder and curiosity as he staggered up the aisle after coming back from the other side of the Barrier the last time. Danny had *seen* him come back. He'd completely forgotten that! Finding Anna Varga had driven everything else out of his mind. But Danny had seen him coming back. Danny had come to this TV set to investigate. The golf ball was proof of that. And Claire. Claire had been coming to find Danny. She would have followed. . . .

And they weren't waiting at the clock. And the line to the other side of the Barrier had been left open. And the shop assistant had said . . . *disappearing acts.*

Patrick pushed his fist into his mouth to stop himself from calling out. He stuffed the golf ball deep in his pocket and held it there. Claire and Danny had gone through the Barrier! He didn't know how it had happened, but he knew it as surely as he knew his own name. And the Barrier was unstable. The computer was unreliable. They were in terrible danger! He knew what he had to do. He took a deep breath and stepped in front of the TV screen.

"I'm ready," he said, through clenched teeth. "Let me through!"

And again, stomach lurching, eyes tightly closed, he crossed the Barrier.

Claire was working shoulder to shoulder with Wendy Minelli, shoveling things back through the huge cracks

that had zigzagged across the Barrier in the last cata-
strophic break. Above their heads women in overalls
were swarming over scaffolding. Objects fell about
Claire like rain, striking her shoulders and back and pil-
ing up on the ground around her. The earth under her
feet was quaking and growling. She could feel the sweat
dripping down her forehead.

Far away up the hill she could hear people calling
out and crying in fear and panic. Danny was up there
somewhere. Her heart ached for him. And her arms and
back ached agonizingly, too, as she bent and pushed,
bent and pushed, over and over again. But if she
stopped, even for a moment, the black-uniformed Agent
barked at her, and Wendy nudged her sharply. "Keep
working!" Wendy urged. "Don't stop! Don't draw attention to yourself, Claire, for goodness' sake."

"What are we doing? What's happening? Where is all
this stuff coming from?" Claire wailed, as a cardigan, a
fluffy slipper, a sun hat, a dog's lead, four odd socks,
and a necklace made of blue shells tumbled into her
arms in a hopeless tangle. She pushed them back
through the gaping hole in front of her. There was a
violent gust of wind, and the Agent's smart black cap
came tumbling down the hill. She grabbed at it in rage,
looked quickly left and right to make sure no one was
watching, and stuffed it into the hole with the other
things. Serve him right!

"Your side," said Wendy briefly. "I'll explain later.
Or Patrick will. Just keep going."

"Your side"? What did she mean? Your side of what?

And what did Patrick have to do with it? Patrick! Claire took a quick look at her watch. Eleven o'clock! He'd be waiting for her and Danny right now, at the Chestnut Tree Village Clock. Oh, what a mess!

Patrick opened his eyes and blinked. Where was he? A dark and silent place. Hard floor beneath his feet. Vague shapes looming up around him. And it was cold. He shivered. He began to feel his way around, hands stretched out in front of him, and then froze. Somewhere a door was opening. There were voices. Someone was coming. He had to hide! His hands, flailing around desperately, found the edge of something hard and high. He felt his way behind the object and crouched down, holding his breath.

One, two, three clicks, and light flooded the room. Bright, white light. Patrick shaded his dazzled eyes with his hand and drew a startled breath. He knew where he was now. In the "Finders Keepers" studio. The set was still in place. In front were the rows of chairs where the audience sat. Over at the side was the bench where the Seekers, Eleanor Doon, Clyde O'Brien, and Wendy Minelli, had sat. And the high thing he was hiding behind was Lucky Lamont's prize wheel. It was all exactly the same. But deserted, like a ghost town.

Footsteps sounded on the hard, shiny floor. Patrick shrank back in his hiding place.

"We'll be okay here for a while," shrilled a familiar voice. "Now, Max . . ."

Patrick peeped out from behind the wheel. Relief

flooded through him. He jumped up. "Boopie!" he shouted. "Max! Estelle!"

The three of them fell back in shock, their mouths open, their eyes wide with fright.

Boopie was the first to recover. "Patrick!" she squealed. "Where did you spring from? Oh, you gave me such a *fright*!"

"Fright!" growled Max. "Fright's not the word for it. You scared me half to death!"

"Patrick." Estelle was pale and worried-looking. "You shouldn't have come. I'm sorry we weren't there to receive your message. They've put a guard on the computer-room door. They won't let us in. They're still saying the Barrier's going to sort itself out, that they don't really think it's 'Finders Keepers,' but I think they're suspicious all the same. And they're not taking any risks. We came here to try to work out what to do. But we didn't dream you'd . . ."

"Did you find the clockmaker?" demanded Max. "Do we know what's wrong with the clock?"

Patrick nodded. He held out the plans Anna Varga had given him. "One of the regulators is missing," he said, as Max took the paper and began unfolding it. "It's a little bird. It must have fallen off last Saturday, when the clock got shaken up. The clockmaker had a heart attack or something when it happened. She's still in the hospital now. I saw her there. Her name's Anna Varga."

Boopie clapped her hands together. "Patrick, you did it!"

Max and Estelle exchanged glances. Boopie was smiling proudly.

"That's fantastic, boy," said Max. "Now. The bird might be somewhere underneath. . . ."

"Oh, we found the bird," said Patrick awkwardly. "My sister, Claire, found it this morning."

"What?"

"Yes. She put it in her bag. She was going to hand it in on our way out."

"Well . . ." Max tugged at his hair, trying desperately to keep his voice calm and even. "Well, Patrick, dear boy, why are you here? Why aren't you over there, getting the bird from Claire and putting it *back?*"

"Because," said Patrick, looking dully at their expectant faces. "Because Claire's over *here*, Max. While I was with Anna Varga she came through the TV, through the channel you left open. With my little brother. She's here. Somewhere. And the bird's here with her."

The others stared at him, then at one another. In a group they moved forward, and Estelle opened her arms. Patrick ran into them, burying his face in her shoulder. "Estelle, what will I do?" he sobbed. "Where are they? The computer could've dumped them anywhere. And Danny's so little. And Claire's got the bird. And soon it'll be twelve o'clock, and . . ."

She held him close and patted his back gently. "We'll find them, dear heart. Don't you worry. You leave it to us now." Her words were calm, but he heard the fear in her voice and felt her shaking slightly as she held him. He knew that she, too, was thinking of Danny, terrified in a strange place.

"We'll split up," said Boopie quickly. "I'll check this part of the studio building, because I can't go outside without being recognized. Estelle can do the cafeteria and the offices and all that part, because they know her there and won't be suspicious if she wanders around. And Max and Patrick can check outside, down by the Barrier. The computer put Patrick there once, remember? It might have done the same trick again this time. All right?"

Estelle and Max nodded. Patrick pulled gently away from Estelle and looked from one to the other. His heart sank. He could tell from their grave faces that neither of them believed there was time left to do anything. They would go along with Boopie's plan only because they couldn't bear not to do anything at all. Not because they thought there was any chance of success.

"Come on, then," cried Boopie brightly. She led the way out of the studio. "We'll meet back here at ten to twelve if not before. All right?" Patrick saw that tears were glittering in her eyes. But she went on smiling. She gave Estelle a little push as she went through the door. "Cheer up, sis. It's not the end of the world!" She paused. "Well, not yet, anyway!" she added, and lifted her chin. "Take care, all," she whispered. "And good finding!"

15

LOSERS WEEPERS

The trembling of the earth stopped, as quickly as it had begun, and Danny dropped to his knees. Only then did he remember the little china bird. He'd put it down on the grass back there, and then he'd run away, leaving it behind. A wave of horror washed over him. What if he couldn't find it again? He couldn't bear it! He began trotting back the way he'd come, scanning the ground. The wind tore at his clothes and hair, and thunder still sounded from the bottom of the hill. But Danny noticed none of it. His thoughts were fixed on that little blue-and-yellow object that to him meant comfort in this awful place.

He looked up. Surely by now he was almost back where he'd started from. And then he skidded to a halt. Ahead of him was a tall, thin woman, standing quite still, looking at the ground. As he watched, she slowly bent down and put out a long arm, jangling with brace-lets, to pluck something from a clump of grass. Danny's heart gave a double thump. Oh, no! He began to call out, but before the words had left his mouth the woman had straightened up. In her hand was the bird. She ex-amined it closely. Then she nodded to herself with satisfaction, stuffed the bird into her pocket, and began to make her way up the hill.

Danny ran after her, as fast as he could. In a minute he was beside her. He tugged at her flapping skirt. "Please!" he called.

The woman stopped and stared down at him. Danny dropped her skirt hastily. She looked like a witch. Her hollow gray eyes stared blankly from a crabby-looking face. Her hair was scraped back into a tight bun stuck with pins, and dozens and dozens of chains hung round her neck.

"What do you want?" the woman said in a harsh voice.

"You—um—you've got my bird," stuttered Danny, eyes wide with fright. "The bird you picked up. It's mine."

The woman grabbed greedily at her pocket, holding it tightly shut. Her fingers were covered in rings, Danny saw. Why would anyone want so many rings? They winked and shone, and when you looked at them one by one they seemed quite pretty. But crammed all together like that they made her hands look ugly. "Finders keepers," she mumbled. "Losers weepers." She turned her back on Danny and hurried away.

Danny stood helplessly for a moment and then ran to catch up with her. Again he tugged at her skirt. "It's mine!" he shouted. "Please give it back!" But this time the woman made no answer. She just pushed his hand away, and kept walking.

Danny followed. The woman looked over her shoulder once or twice, and saw him. And each time she did, she pressed her hand to her pocket and walked on, a little faster than before. But Danny went on following. His legs were sore and his shoulder hurt. But he wanted his bird back. And also, actually, he didn't know what else to do. He had to do something, and somewhere underneath his fear and tiredness was the vague idea that this woman could help him. "Finders keepers," she had said. She must know all about the game. Maybe she could show him how to get home. So Danny followed.

Keeping his distance, he followed her up the hill and along a road, and up to a big old house standing all by itself behind a high wall. He followed her through the broken, rusty iron gates and up the drive where grass, weeds, and ivy tangled together on a bed of little red stones.

The woman reached the front steps of the house and looked over her shoulder again. She seemed almost scared to see Danny standing on the drive. "Get away!" she called, waving a hand at him. "Get off! Or I'll have the Agents on you!"

Danny kept walking. The woman backed away, clutching her pocket. She pulled out a key that hung on a long chain around her neck and bent to fumble with the front door lock. Danny climbed the steps and stood watching her.

The key turned in the lock and the tall door creaked open. Without even thinking about it, Danny sprang forward, ducked under the key chain between the door

and the woman's bent body, and wriggled through the opening into the house. The woman made a strangled sound. It was half a shout of rage and half a cry of fear. She struggled to pull the key from the lock to free herself and, finally succeeding, flung herself after him. The door slammed behind her with an echoing crash.

Danny and the woman stood facing each other, panting, in a huge, dim, square hallway. Doors led off from each side to rooms beyond. Dark, musty-smelling rooms. Despite the dimness and his fright, Danny could see that the hall was lined with dozens of shelves and cabinets, each crammed with silver, china, and glass objects: statues and plates, cups and ornaments, fans and vases, little boxes and big boxes, and pictures in silver frames. All sorts of stuff. In fact, he'd never seen so much stuff in one place before. He looked around in awe. As a collector himself, he found this room very interesting.

The woman's voice broke into his thoughts. "Who are you?" she demanded, holding tightly to her pocket. "Why did you follow me?" She pointed a shaking finger at him. "You want to rob me, don't you? Don't you?"

Danny stared at her. "No," he said simply. "I just want my bird. That's not robbing. I found it. It's mine."

"*I* found it," snapped the woman. "You left it. I found it. Now it's mine."

"That's not fair! I didn't mean to leave it!" shouted Danny, suddenly angry as well as frightened. He looked around the crowded hallway. "Anyway, you've got . . . you've got millions of things. You don't need my bird.

But *I* need it. It's my prize. From 'Finders Keepers.' You know."

"'Finders Keepers'?" The woman frowned suspiciously. Her hand left her pocket and folded itself protectively over the fingers of her other hand. "What do you mean, 'You know'? Did 'Finders Keepers' send you here?"

Suddenly she drew back. She clasped her hands to her chest, hiding them from him. "That's it, isn't it?" she shouted. "'Finders Keepers' sent you. To take back the ring! I saw that other boy, the Finder, down by the Barrier fence. They've brought him back. He found my ring for me, but now they want it back, don't they? That's their little game. They want my ring." Her hands shook as she pressed them to her.

"Or maybe there's more to it than that," she went on. "Maybe they want *all* my rings. Is that it? They saw them on me, and now they want them all. They're nothing but a gang of thieves. That's it, isn't it?"

Danny had had enough. He backed away from her. "I'm not thieves! I don't want rings," he wailed. "I want to go home! I want my mummy!" He dropped down on the marble floor and burst into tears.

The woman blinked. She stood quite still and watched him for a moment. Then she unclenched her fists and thoughtfully rubbed her mouth with her hand. Her brow wrinkled.

Danny cried on. He couldn't try to be brave anymore. He cried for his home, and his parents, and for Claire and Patrick. He cried because he was lonely and frightened and lost. And he was in a crazy woman's house. And no one would help him.

A foot nudged his leg. "Take it, then," a voice said.

Danny looked up, sobbing. The woman was standing, frowning, over him, holding out the little china bird. She jerked her hand impatiently. "Take it," she said again.

Danny put up his hand and took the bird. He rubbed his fingers over its smooth, round body and held it up to his hot cheek. It was cool and comforting. His sobbing quieted. His thumb stole into his mouth. He rocked slowly to and fro. His eyes closed.

"You're lost," the woman said almost wonderingly, as if she'd just discovered something amazing.

Danny kept his eyes closed. That way he couldn't see her or this strange house. He couldn't see how lost he really was.

"You don't have to cry. They'll look for you," the woman went on, still in that quiet voice. "Your parents will, won't they?"

Danny's eyes opened. He took his thumb out of his mouth. "And Claire," he said.

"Who's Claire?"

"My sister. She'll look for me. And Patrick will, too."

"My brother got lost," the woman said dreamily. "I was just remembering. Johnnie got lost once. When we were kids. I was supposed to be looking after him. But he wandered off and got lost in the bush at the back of the house. There were gullies there, then. And snakes. And a creek. We looked for him the whole afternoon."

"Did he get finded?" asked Danny, with a last, shuddering sob.

"Yes." The woman almost smiled. "Dad and I found him. He was sitting under a tree, crying. Like you were crying just then. That's what made me think of it. You looked like him, for a minute. He was crying, sucking his thumb. Poor little boy." She looked over Danny's head, remembering. "We were so happy when we found him. We took him home. Then Mother cried. We had ice cream for dinner. Even me. And it was all my fault."

"Is Johnnie here now?" Danny looked around the echoing hallway, as if expecting to see a little boy emerge from one of the doorways.

"No. No one's here," the woman sighed. "That was a long time ago. No one's here now, except me. And my things." She looked around, her eyes lingering on the crowded cupboards and shelves.

"They're nice," said Danny, wiping his eyes and peering up at her.

She nodded slowly, still looking around her. "I don't bother with people. I just look after my things now." She paused. "Things don't die," she added strangely. "They don't leave you. They're always the same. Better than people."

Danny bit his lip. It seemed to him that this wasn't true at all, but he thought if he said so she might get angry again, so he said nothing. He didn't want her to get angry. He wanted her to stay gentle. Because he wanted her to help him.

16

Two Out of Three

"Keep close to me," Max warned Patrick as they reached the brow of the hill. "We've got to be careful. Especially with that Doon woman hanging around. Looks like she didn't recognize you the first time. When the Agents were questioning us they didn't know you were here, anyway, so no report had been handed in. But we mightn't be so lucky again."

Patrick squinted against the wind and looked down. The hillside swarmed with Barrier-combers. Along the fence stood a double line of Agents, sticks held high. Down by the Barrier, red-coated Barrier Guards worked feverishly, while objects piled in great heaps around them.

"Can you see them?" asked Max.

Patrick strained his eyes, trying to find two familiar figures in the crowd. "Not so far," he said at last. "We'd better go farther down."

They moved down toward the fence. As they drew closer they could hear the restless muttering of the crowd clustering behind it.

"Let us through, you morons," shouted an old man with snow-white hair and a Santa Claus beard. "The

Guards can't cope. Look at it! Stuff everywhere. Let us through! We'll clean it up for you quick smart."

"Scavengers' rights!" called a woman beside him.

The crowd murmured angry agreement. The murmur grew and spread, like ripples on a pond.

A thin little woman standing beside Patrick stirred uneasily. "I don't like this, Perce," she muttered to her companion. "It's getting ugly again. They're getting ready for something. And I keep thinking about that last break. The way the ground shook. It's not safe here. Let's go home."

The man she was speaking to pulled his red-and-blue-striped woolly hat more firmly over his forehead. "You're right. Should've kept away after the last time, I reckon," he said. "Okay, love. Hold tight. Don't want to lose you, do I?"

They grinned at each other, linked arms, and began to push their way through the crowd back up the hill.

Patrick looked desperately from right to left, but he still couldn't see Claire or Danny. Just a sea of bodies and grim, mischievous, scared or intent faces, eyes fixed on the Barrier.

Danny finished the glass of water the woman had brought him and gave a sigh of contentment. He'd been so thirsty. He looked up at her. "Can you take me home now?" he asked confidently.

She stared at him, frowning. "Oh, I can't do anything like that," she said slowly.

"Why not?" Danny pressed his lips together hard, so as not to start crying again.

"I just can't. I—I've got too much to do," said the woman, clasping and unclasping her hands. "You can get home by yourself. I've got my things to see to. You get along now." She turned and strode to the door. She pulled it open. "Get along now," she repeated. "Go home."

"Please!" Danny looked at her beseechingly, his mouth quivering. "I don't know how."

The woman twitched her head from side to side as if trying to get rid of some annoying fly or worrying thought.

"Please!" Danny said again.

She looked around helplessly, wanting an easy way out. But the objects on the shelves stood silently under their film of dust. No answer came from there. "Where do you live?" she said finally.

"A-hundred-and-twenty-seven-Beswick-Street-Langley," gabbled Danny. "Or you could bring me to the lost boys' place at the police station. Or you could bring me to Chestnut Tree Village. That's where me and Patrick and Claire were. Where the TV is, that I came through."

"TV?" the woman frowned. She was really confused now.

Danny squeezed his hands together. "Yes, you know," he pleaded. This woman knew about "Finders Keepers," didn't she? So why was she looking at him so strangely? "The TV. The 'Finders Keepers' TV. That you talk to and then it goes dark and you get to that windy place with all the things on the ground. You know!"

"You're not from this side," the woman whispered. She peered at Danny. "They brought you over, too, through the Barrier, like the other one. No wonder the Barrier's breaking up. Everyone knows it's the Finders doing it. And now they've brought two of you. Why did they do that? Disobey orders like that?"

"No one broughted me. I came by myself!" cried poor Danny. "I was naughty to Claire. I'm sorry. I want to go home!" Tears began to gather in his eyes again.

"Now, don't start!" said the woman hastily. She fiddled uncertainly with her rings, twisting them on her fingers. "This changes things. I'll have to do something. I can't leave it like this now. I'll have to report it. Come on."

Danny ran up to her and hugged her legs, through her skirt. "Thank you," he said.

She looked down at him, then at a faded old picture in a silver frame on a table near the door. The picture showed a serious-looking little girl in plaits and a small boy with shining hair and a round face. She looked down at Danny's head again, and her grim face relaxed for a moment. "You'd better tell me your name," she said abruptly. "What's your name?"

"Danny—I mean, Daniel Thomas Minter," said Danny. He dropped his arms and followed the woman out the door. "What's yours?" he added shyly.

"Eleanor. Eleanor Mary Doon," said the woman.

Danny jumped from one step to another and stood on the veranda while the woman locked her door, testing it once, twice, three times. "Can we go now?" he pleaded at last. "Can we go home, Eleanor?"

Her eyes shifted. "Come on," she said in a flat voice.

Danny and Eleanor Doon walked away from the big locked house, down the long ivy-choked driveway and on to the road beyond the gates. After a while, Danny took her hand.

"Now!"

It was impossible to tell where the shout had come from, but on the signal hundreds of Barrier-combers pressing against the fence reacted as one. They pushed forward violently, flattening it with a single thrust. Scattering the fearsome-looking Agents by their sheer numbers, they pounded down the hill.

Patrick and Max were forced to run with them. It was that or be crushed. Down toward the Barrier they stumbled, concentrating only on keeping their feet. In front of them they could see the lines of Barrier Guards turning to face them, their hands full of the objects they were battling to return to the other side. But it was obviously a battle they weren't winning. They all stood knee-deep in tangled heaps of things. Their exhausted faces were evidence of the hopelessness of their task.

One Guard turned more slowly than the others. Her face was pale. Her long hair fell untidily over the collar of a red jacket that seemed too big for her. And under

the jacket she was wearing jeans. Patrick looked at her.
Saw her face change, her mouth open. He yelled with
shocked joy.

"Claire!"

"Patrick!"

They flew into each other's arms.

17

Hide-and-Seek

"Patrick!" cried Claire, holding her brother tightly. "Oh, Patrick, what are you doing here? Oh, I'm so glad to see you." Then she pulled away. "I've lost Danny," she whispered. "Patrick, Wendy's told me about 'Finders Keepers' and everything. I could hardly believe it. But we're here—it must be true! Danny came through the TV set and I came after him. And I saw him, walking up there near the fence, but I couldn't get to him, and . . ."

Max and Wendy Minelli moved around to shield them from the curious eyes of the people nearby. "Keep your voices down," ordered Wendy, casting a worried glance behind her. "Nothing's changed, Claire. If anyone works out who you and your brother are, or where you came from, the Agents'll be on to you both."

"Patrick, the bird," Max reminded him in an undertone. "We haven't got time to waste."

Patrick tried to pull himself together. His knees and hands were shaking violently. He stiffened himself all over, to stop them. "Claire, where's your bag?" he said hurriedly.

She stared at him. "In Wendy's hut. But . . ."

"We've got to get it. Quickly."

Wendy glanced around her again, thinking fast. Agents, Barrier-combers, and Guards were milling all around them, scuffling and dodging as the officials tried to drive the invaders back.

She put her hand firmly on Patrick's shoulder. He jumped in surprise. "Come on, you!" she said in a loud voice. "You're not getting away this time! Claire! Take the other one."

Claire blinked once. Wendy nodded at her, frowning. Immediately Claire understood. She pushed Max forward. "Get going!" she ordered.

They marched together toward Wendy's hut. No one interfered with them, or even looked twice. Two scruffy Barrier-combers being escorted away by two Barrier Guards. Nothing unusual about that.

"Wait here!" barked Wendy as they reached the red hut. She darted inside and came out with Claire's shoulder bag. She thrust it into Patrick's hands. He pushed his hand inside, felt around, and then looked up at them, dismayed.

"It's gone!"

"What's gone?" demanded Claire. "Someone tell me what's going on!"

"The little china bird. Off the clock!" Patrick was panic-stricken. "It's important. We need it. Where is it?"

"In the bag, where I put it!" Claire retorted. She

snatched the bag from him and felt inside. Her irritation changed to confusion. "It's gone," she said. "But how— oh, I know! It must have fallen out when the bag tipped over. At the back of the hut. Come on!"

They hurried to the spot and searched the grass. Nothing. Wendy finally shook her head. "A Scavenger's got it, for sure. They've been picking the ground all around here. It'll probably turn up for sale on a stall later."

Max looked at his watch. His face was gray and old-looking. "There won't *be* a later if we can't find it in the next fifteen minutes," he said. "The Barrier won't be able to stand the twelve o'clock strike."

Wendy sprang into action. "I don't understand any of this, but if the birdie's that important we'll just have to find it, won't we?" she said crisply. "Come on, prisoners! We'll get you up to the fence and then you can spread the word we want it. Ruby'll help, if you can find her. You'll have to offer a reward, of course. A big fat one. Is that all right?"

"Anything," said Max, and bowed his head.

"Okay," Wendy said. "Off we go then."

She and Claire took up their positions again and marched Patrick and Max off between them. They hurried up the hill. Around them strode other Guards and a sprinkling of Agents, driving Barrier-combers before them.

At the fence Wendy stopped. Agents stood shoulder to shoulder along the damaged section. She frowned ferociously at Patrick and Max. "Get between them, you," she told Claire in a loud voice. "You can take them on alone. I have to go back to my post. Don't take any smart talk, and don't let them get away."

"Yes, sir!" Claire hurried to obey. Patrick and Max kept their eyes down, but Patrick could feel the glare of the Agents' eyes on him.

"Watch it, all of you," said Wendy. Her voice was harsh, but Claire, Patrick, and Max knew she was saying good-bye and take care, in the only way she could.

"Yes, sir!" Claire answered for them all in the only way *she* could. "Thank you, sir!" She pulled at Max and Patrick's arms. "Come on, you two," she said roughly. "Let's go."

They marched up to the fence. The Agents, eyes blank behind their black sunglasses, stood firm for a moment, then moved aside to let them through. They marched on, through a scattered crowd of jeering Barrier-combers. They didn't look back. No one tried to stop them. "Claire, can you see Danny anywhere?" asked Patrick after a moment.

"No," she whispered. "And listen, what will we do about spreading the word about the bird and the reward and everything?"

"Wait till we're a bit away from the fence," said Max. "Then we'll see."

They strode on for a moment, then slowed and came to a halt. They were nearly at the top of the hill. There were no Agents here. Just groups of Barrier-combers sitting on the grass as though they were having a picnic, the objects they'd just taken from around the Barrier spread out in front of them.

"Fools," said Max bitterly. "Worrying about that stuff when everything's coming down around their ears. Time's running out. Literally. How can they even think about their stupid little free bits and pieces? Fools!"

"They're not fools, Max," said Patrick, watching the people sitting hunched in the wind, looking at their finds. "They're only doing what they always do, aren't they? They don't know how serious things are. Only we know."

Max sighed. "You're right. What's the point of being angry with them? *I'm* the fool!"

It was getting darker. The sky was almost black. Patrick shivered as the wind bit through his sweat-soaked T-shirt. He scanned the groups of people, looked farther up the hill. And then he saw her. Ruby was standing looking down at the Barrier, her cardigan wrapped around her, her skirt flying backward, her white hair wild. "Come on!" Patrick yelped. "Up there!"

He pulled the others with him up the hill. Alarmed, Ruby watched them come. As they reached her she primmed her mouth and jerked her head in Patrick's direction. "You could give the kid a break, couldn't you, mate?" she said to Claire, carefully casual. "Go on! Leave him with me. I'll see he doesn't get into trouble again."

"It's okay, Ruby," Patrick said softly. "This isn't really

a Guard. It's my sister, Claire. Wendy fixed her up with a Guard's coat."

The old woman's face broke into a delighted smile. "Well, trust Wendy to come up with the goods," she chortled. "You had me going all right. When I saw you trailing up with a red-coat between you I thought you'd been done for sure." Then the grin faded. She turned on Max. "You got two of them here now, have you? The kid *and* his sister," she accused. "What do you think you're playing at, you nut case?"

"It was a mistake, Ruby," Patrick explained quickly, before Max could retort. "And, look, we need help, really fast. We've lost something. Down by the Barrier."

He told her about the bird. She listened carefully.

"I'll spread the word," she promised. "Reward, huh? That ought to do it. Might take a bit of time, though."

"Time's just what we haven't got, Ruby," Max put in. He glanced at his watch.

"Five minutes," Ruby said. "Have we got that long?"

Sweat was glistening on Max's forehead. "Just."

The old Barrier-comber turned to go, but Patrick stopped her. "One more thing, Ruby," he said. "Our little brother Danny's here somewhere."

"A little boy in a blue T-shirt and shorts," Claire added. "He's got fair hair. He's four."

"Yeah?" Ruby looked thoughtful. "Look," she said, after a moment. "I don't want to worry you for nothing. It might be some other kid. But I've been home for a cuppa and on the way back I passed the Channel 8 building, and I did see a boy dressed like that. Near the door."

"You did?" Patrick and Claire stared at each other, hope rising in a wave and flowing between them.

"Yeah," said Ruby. "Thing is, he wasn't alone." She looked gravely at Max. "Loony Doon was with him," she said. "Eleanor Doon. She was trying to get him inside, I reckon."

"What?" Patrick and Max exclaimed in horror. Claire didn't understand what was going on, but she saw the fear on their faces, and pressed her hand to her mouth.

"We'll have to go. Now!" said Max. "If she gets to the Agents with him, we've had it."

"What about the bird, then?" demanded the old woman.

Max thought hard for a second. "If you get the bird in the next five minutes, Ruby, bring it to Channel 8. Someone'll be waiting at the door." He took a step away, then paused and turned back. "And Ruby," he said carefully, "if you haven't found the bird in five minutes, I want you to do something else for me. I want you to forget the bird, and us, and get away from here as fast as you can. And take as many of your mates with you as will go. It's going to get rough."

Her faded eyes summed him up. She glanced down at the Barrier again and pursed her lips. "Bad as that, is it?" she said. "After all these years. The signs were all there, but I couldn't believe it." Her shoulders sagged. Then she shrugged them back and looked up at Max.

"Thanks for the warning, sonny," she said jauntily. "I'll tell the others. But I reckon I'll hang around. If the Barrier goes, we're all done for, in the long run. So I may as well see the fireworks. Go with a bang, as they say."

Patrick put out his hand to her, but she waved him away. "Get along with all of you!" she said roughly. "Get about your business, and I'll get about mine! See you in the spring!" She turned and made off, bending determinedly into the wind.

18

Countdown

"Now," puffed Max as they jogged up the road that led to the TV studio. "You kids listen to me. Especially you, Patrick. You've both been great. But now it's time for you to leave things to us. You've done all you can. If we're quick we can still get the two of you back home before twelve o'clock. It'll be a near thing, but we can just do it."

"The three of us, you mean," said Patrick. "You've forgotten about Danny."

Max didn't answer. The other two looked quickly at him. He ran on, clumsily, like someone not used to running, staring straight ahead.

"We're not going without Danny, you know," warned Claire.

Max still didn't look around. "You might have to," he muttered.

Claire and Patrick both stopped dead. Max faltered, then he also stopped. The children shook their heads.

"No way," Patrick said firmly. "No way, Max."

"Don't even think about it," added Claire.

Max regarded them helplessly.

"Come on." Patrick started to run again. "We're nearly there. Look out for Danny." The blood was starting to pound in his head. He'll be there, he thought. He'll be there. He must be there. Waiting by the door, with or without Eleanor Doon. We can't go without him. We can't. He concentrated on that. He tried not to think about the lost bird, the regulator for the Chestnut Tree Village clock, and the terrible disaster that was going to befall them all if it wasn't returned to its rightful place. There was no point in thinking about that. No point. Max would have to handle that. Yet Ruby's words kept coming back to him. *If the Barrier goes, we're all done for, in the long run.* He was the Finder. They had relied on him. And he'd failed them.

The door to the TV studio was in sight. And, as before, a crowd of Barrier-combers surrounded it. But the crowd was bigger now. And angrier. And hovering on its fringes, right in front of them, holding tightly to a tall, thin woman's hand was—

"Danny!" Claire's shriek of joy filled Patrick's ears. He saw his sister spring forward, run faster than he'd ever seen her run. He saw Danny pull away from Eleanor Doon and race to meet her, leaping into her arms.

"Oh, thank you, thank you, thank you!" Patrick found he was whispering the words over and over again. And then he could hear them being said aloud. By Claire. Claire was sobbing them to Eleanor Doon, looking at her over Danny's fair head, tears running down her cheeks. "Oh, thank you, thank you, thank you!"

Eleanor Doon didn't answer. Different expressions

were passing over her face as she watched Danny's clutching arms and Claire's tears.

Max was watching her nervously. "Get going!" he ordered Claire and Patrick. "We've got to get to the computer room."

"They won't let you through. I've been trying," said Eleanor Doon, in her curiously toneless voice. She smiled thinly.

"We'll see about that," said Max. "Patrick, Claire,

stay close together. Hold on to Danny." He moved to the edge of the crowd. "Let us through, please," he bawled, trying to push a path through the people. "We're on official business. Look!" He pointed to Claire, bedraggled and crying but still in her red jacket. "We've got a Guard with us."

"Big deal!" sneered a curly-haired woman in front of him. She linked arms with the people on either side of her, blocking Max's way. "No one in or out. That's flat. Channel 8's the cause of our troubles. We're giving them some. That's fair, isn't it?"

"You'll be sorry for this," warned Max, his eyes shifting from one face to another. "There are Agents inside this building!"

"Not anymore, matey. Or only one or two. The rest of them took off down to the Barrier," said the man on the curly-haired woman's left. "They're in a frenzy. They've finally decided we were right about 'Finders Keepers.' No more talk about the Barrier fixing itself up now. It's going bye-bye." He jerked his thumb back at the TV building. "And this place here's to blame."

"Give up. They won't let you through," said Eleanor Doon in Max's ear.

He spun around to face her, his face beaded with sweat. "I've got to get these kids in! I've got to get them home to their parents! Now. Or it'll be too late. Whatever happens, they should be together." He gripped her arm. Max, the cool, calm one who knew all the answers, was pleading now. With the most unlikely person. "Please!" he begged Eleanor Doon. "Think of something! Help me!"

She stared at him in amazement. For the second time today, someone was asking her for help. *Her.* The woman they called Loony Doon. The woman who'd forgotten about people. Who'd given them up because caring and loving hurt too much. Didn't he know that asking *her* for help was pointless and ridiculous? She stared at Patrick, and at Claire, and at Danny, who turned his tear-stained face toward her just at that moment. And Danny smiled at her, his thumb in his mouth.

For a second their eyes locked.

Then Eleanor Doon clutched at her chest as if, almost as if, something inside her had cracked. And she straightened her shoulders, raised herself to her full height, held up her arms. And she shouted. "Look!" she yelled, her voice breaking with the effort. "Look here!" She waited for a moment while the crowd turned to stare, pointing and tittering at her.

And then, as if it was happening in slow motion, Patrick saw her begin to pull at the rings on her fingers. Saw her drag them off in twos and threes and fours. Saw her fling them high, in handfuls, so they scattered behind her in the dust. Dozens of them, glittering and bright. Saw the Barrier-combers scatter, shrieking, to pounce on them, leaving a clear, open path to the door. Heard Eleanor Doon's voice. "Go!" She was shouting to him, to them. "Go home!"

And then the door was opening, and Boopie and Estelle were calling, and he was running, with Claire and Danny and Max beside him. And they were tumbling inside. And the door was slamming behind them.

"Did you see that? Did you see what she did?" They were running again, down a deserted corridor. At the end two other corridors led off left and right. They were

nearly at the computer room. But Patrick couldn't stop talking. "Boopie, Estelle, did you see . . . ?"

"I couldn't believe it," answered Boopie. "No one would have believed it."

"Keep it down, you two," grunted Max. He slowed to a walk and the others did the same. They crept together, not speaking, to the end of the corridor. Max peered around the corner to the right, then drew back quickly. "There's still an Agent on the door," he muttered. "Rats!"

"Rats?" Danny piped up with interest.

"Sshh, Danny." Claire let go of his hand and hurriedly smoothed back her hair, tucking it behind her ears and under her jacket collar. "Wait here," she said. "I'll fix this." She lifted her chin and strolled around the corner, raising her hand to the black-uniformed figure by the computer-room door.

They saw her speaking to him and pointing down the corridor, away from them. He nodded, glanced at his watch, and marched off briskly. Claire took his place, her back to the door, staring straight ahead. After a moment she turned her head to make sure the coast was clear, then looked back to their corner and beckoned. They ran to join her.

"I told him I was sent to relieve him," she said smugly. "He's gone to have a cup of tea."

Estelle clapped her on the back. "Good on you, Claire!"

"In!" said Max.

They crowded into the computer room. Danny and

Claire looked around, wide-eyed. "Wow," breathed Danny respectfully.

"Stand there and hold still," ordered Max. "We'll have to work fast." He raced to the computer. "The fix is holding," he said, his eyes darting over the screen. "Now . . ." His hand moved forward.

"Max, Max, stop!" called Patrick. "Stop! Listen! We haven't got the bird. We can't fix the clock. What are we going to do?"

Danny tugged at Claire's sleeve. "Do you want to see what I found, Claire?"

Claire squeezed his hand. "Later, Danny," she said softly. "When we're home." She exchanged worried glances with Estelle. "Patrick—" she began. But Max was talking again.

"I told you, Patrick, there's no more time. I've got to send you back before the twelve o'clock strike, or I mightn't *ever* be able to get you back."

"But if the clock isn't fixed our side's in as much trouble as yours, Max," cried Patrick. "Send Danny and Claire back. I'll wait here for Ruby. She'll have found the bird by now. For sure. Then . . ."

"No!" barked Max. "No! It's too late!"

"*I've* got a bird, you know, Claire," said Danny brightly.

"Have you, Danny? That's nice." Claire glanced again at Estelle. Then she bent down and picked the little boy up. "Hold tight, now," she said. She put her other arm around Patrick and held him close. She was trembling with anxiety. She looked straight at Max, and nodded. His hand moved forward again.

But Danny was wriggling, fumbling in his pocket, dragging out something. "See, Claire?" he insisted, holding up a blue-and-yellow object that blurred in front of her eyes. "I lost my golf ball, but this is nice. It feels the same in my pocket. Round and heavy, see?"

"*Danny!*" Patrick and Claire's shout echoed in the tiny room. Boopie, Estelle, and Max gasped. Danny looked from face to astonished face and beamed. He'd never ever had such a satisfying reaction to one of his finds before.

"It's my prize. I found it," he repeated happily. "At 'Finders Keepers.'"

"He had it all along!" shrieked Boopie. "I don't believe it!"

Max was tearing at his hair in excitement. "Patrick!" he yelled. "You've just got time. You can do it, boy! Ready?"

"Wait, Max! The plans!" shouted Estelle. "Give Patrick the clock plans, in case . . ."

"Aagh!" Max bounded across the room, tearing the bulky paper from his pocket. He thrust it at Patrick. "I'm going nuts!" he roared. Then he slapped his forehead. "And quickly, someone!" He began darting around the room, shoveling papers to the floor, pulling out drawers, and opening cupboard doors. "He needs something to stick the bird to its socket. Sticky tape or something. Anything! Oh, quickly!"

"Chewing gum!" Boopie pulled out her packet and ran over to Patrick with it. She unwrapped two pieces and popped them into his mouth. He started chewing madly.

"Chewing gum! Yes! Brilliant!" yelled Max, as though he'd never said a word against the stuff in his life. "Now go, kids, go!"

"Hold tight!" shouted Boopie and Estelle together.

The children shut their eyes and clutched one another as if their lives depended on it. Patrick heard Danny gasp, felt Claire shudder. He knew this was it. He knew everything now depended on him. He knew that on the other side he would have to move faster than he'd ever moved in his life. And then his head began to spin, and he knew nothing at all.

19
ZERO HOUR

Patrick opened his eyes. The bright lights were dazzling. His chest was bursting. He breathed out in a shuddering gasp and became aware of Danny and Claire panting beside him. He staggered slowly to his feet. He was in the department store, beside the TV set. He'd come back across the Barrier. An urgent feeling was stabbing through his vague confusion. There was something he had to do. Something important. But what? What did he have to do? He looked at his hand. He was holding a thick paper. The plans of the clock. He blinked. His head cleared. He remembered!

"Quick!" He grabbed Danny's hand. "Claire, we've got to get to the clock! Danny, we have to put the bird back on the clock. It's not your prize. It belongs on the clock. I'll give you your golf ball in a minute, to make up for it, okay?" He took the bird from Danny's chubby paw and began dragging his brother and sister along with him up the aisle toward the door.

"Hey, you kids!" The shop assistant who'd told Patrick off before met them at the end of the aisle. "Didn't I tell you . . . ?"

"Sorry!" gabbled Patrick, darting past him. "No time!"

They raced toward the clock. There was a strange humming noise in Patrick's ears. He shook his head, but the humming went on. Then he realized that the noise wasn't in his head at all. It was coming from the clock. It filled the air: an ominous, rising sound like a million angry bees. The white fence was surrounded by people, murmuring and confused. All of them were staring, fascinated, at the clock's minute hand. It was trembling before the hour. The humming noise grew louder. The ground began to shudder, very slightly. A few people screamed.

Patrick and Claire pushed through the crowd to the fence, pulling Danny between them, ignoring grunts of protest and angry looks. The trembling in the ground grew stronger. The clock's ticking was like a drum—fast, hard, and frightening. The humming noise rose to an almost unbearable pitch. People covered their ears and stepped back, treading on each other's toes. "Earthquake!" a man shouted.

Patrick looked up. He didn't need Anna Varga's plans. He knew where the missing bird should go. But its hole was high up in the painted branches of the chestnut tree. Higher than he'd remembered.

"Neither of us can reach. You'll have to lift me!" he yelled to Claire.

They clambered over the fence, hauling Danny after them. No one called after them or tried to stop them. The clock ticked faster. The ground shook. A small crack began to run up the center of the tree.

"I'm scared, Claire!" Danny cried. "It's like 'Finders Keepers' here. It's all shaking. And the clock's too loud." He sank to the ground and covered his ears.

Claire bent down at the base of the tree and Patrick climbed up on her shoulders. She staggered to her feet, and he took the chewing gum from his mouth and reached up to the place where the missing bird usually popped out of its hole to sing. He still couldn't reach. He raised himself to his knees, feeling Claire's shoulders wobbling underneath him. He stretched his arms as high as they would go, straining every muscle, reaching higher and higher till the tips of his fingers just reached the opening. He pressed his head against the surface of the tree and felt for the metal cup in which the bird sat.

The humming noise filled his head; the ticking of the clock seemed to beat at him, taking his breath away. His fingers were trembling and slippery with sweat. A whirring noise began, deep in the clock's heart. He knew what that meant. It was about to strike. The huge minute hand began to move above him.

He could feel the cup now. He stuck the gum into it and began to slide the little bird into position. Nearly . . . nearly . . .

CLANG! The clock struck, with a jarring, hideous clash of sound. The cup shot out from under Patrick's fingers. He swayed on Claire's shoulders, grabbing at the flat surface of the tree, struggling frantically to keep upright. The bird flew from his grasp and fell. Fell. And hit the tiles. And shattered into a hundred pieces.

Claire and Danny's screams echoed in Patrick's ears. The little cup, still empty, shot back into its hole. The ground rumbled, and with a crash a pane of glass fell from a shop window and smashed. More people screamed, and children began to cry. The blacksmith raised his hammer again.

Patrick hung on the clock, staring down at the pow-
dered fragments, white, blue and yellow, on the tiles
below. He couldn't believe what had happened. He
couldn't take it in. Thoughts and pictures flashed on
and off in his head. Everything was lost. Finished. The
Barrier, Estelle, Max, Boopie, Ruby, the Barrier-combers, Eleanor Doon, "Finders Keepers," Anna Varga,
and in the end everyone here—all these people, Claire,
his parents, Michael, Danny . . .

Danny. Danny's voice, echoing in his mind: *Feels the
same . . . round and heavy . . . in my pocket . . . feels
the . . .*

Patrick's heart thudded. He plunged his hand deep
in his pocket, found what he was looking for, pulled it
out. . . .

CLANG! The cup popped out of its hole again, and
quickly, like lightning, Patrick stuck Danny's golf ball
fast inside it. It fitted perfectly. The clock shuddered.
The cup was pulled back into the hole.

The angry humming stopped. The terrible shaking of
the ground stilled. Patrick waited, exhausted and
trembling. The crowd watched. There was a second's
complete silence. Then the blacksmith raised his hammer again. Brought it down.

And the familiar sweet, rich sound of the Chestnut
Tree Village clock sounded in the air. Once, twice—
and then people began to cheer, and Patrick was tumbling shakily to the ground, and Claire was crying and
Danny was asking questions, and the clock went on
chiming sweetly, calmly, all the way to twelve.

*   *   *

On the other side of the Barrier, Max, Boopie, and Estelle stood huddled on the hillside with Ruby and Eleanor Doon. They clung together, holding each other up on the shaking, rumbling ground. Around them the Barrier-combers who had chosen to wait sat silently, watching. They could hardly see the Barrier now. The sky was black. The raging wind beat in their faces.

Max looked at his watch. "It's time," he said quietly. "Past time. Looks like he didn't make it."

Estelle covered her face with her hands.

"No!" said Boopie. "No! I won't believe it!"

But Ruby said nothing. She had cocked her head, as if listening to something the rest of them couldn't hear.

"Wait!" rasped Eleanor Doon. She was also concentrating, listening, eyes narrowed. "I think . . ."

And as she spoke, at that very moment, the wind died and the ground quieted. An enormous stillness descended over the hillside.

"Max," Boopie whispered fearfully, feeling for Estelle's hand. "Is this . . . ?"

Then a great shout rose up from the Barrier.

"Oh, Boopie, no! It's all right! Look! Look!" cried Estelle, pointing up to the sky.

Like curtains pulling back from a window, the black clouds were parting overhead and sunlight was streaming through. And at the Barrier, Guards and Agents and Barrier Works Squad members were a cheering, leaping mass of red, black, and yellow. The noise they made echoed through the valley and spread up the hill as the

Barrier-combers clambered to their feet and joined in, whooping and dancing. But Boopie, Estelle, Max, Ruby, and Eleanor Doon stood still in the middle of the crowd, silently gripping one another's hands.

"He did it," whispered Estelle at last. "Patrick did it."

Max breathed out. A great, shuddering breath. Then he composed his face and raised his eyebrows. "No reason why he shouldn't, you know," he said coolly. "He had all the necessary equipment."

Ruby snorted. "Hah! Don't pretend you weren't terrified, egghead!" she retorted. "You were as scared as they were."

"Hey, what's this 'they'?" protested Boopie. "You were shaking like a leaf, Ruby. I could feel you. Anyhow, I always knew he'd do it. I *told* you, Estelle, that—"

"Boopie, how can you! You were the one who said . . ."

They argued on for a while, smiling all over their faces.

At the Community Hospital the woman called Elise pushed open the door of room Number 12, carrying a tray. "Here I am, dear," she called brightly. "A nice little bit of lunch for you. Now, today we'll just forget about all our worries, won't we? And eat up like a good . . ." Her voice trailed off. Her mouth dropped open.

The high, white bed was empty.

20

GAME'S END

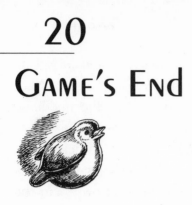

Patrick, Claire, and Danny walked down the shopping-center ramp. Every now and then they turned to one another and grinned. The sky was bright, bright blue. It was hot. Claire took off her jacket. It was pink on this side of the Barrier. Not too bad a color, actually, she thought. Might come in handy when it gets cooler. She looked at the boys walking beside her. They looked appalling! Tattered and filthy. She supposed she did, too. No wonder people were staring.

A very upright, elegant little woman was walking up the ramp toward them, looking at them curiously. Claire put her arms around Patrick and Danny. She wasn't going to care what some stranger thought. After what they'd been through . . .

The woman stopped, watching calmly as they approached. How rude, Claire thought, and looked pointedly away from her.

But Patrick had noticed the stranger, too. And her piercing black eyes made his spine tingle. He'd seen her before. But where?

"Good afternoon, Patrick," the woman greeted him. "Don't you know me?"

He gaped at her. "Anna Varga," he gasped. "But . . . you're sick. You're in the hospital."

She smiled and patted her neatly rolled-up white hair. "Oh, I am quite better now, thanks to you," she said airily. "So I decided to leave that place without further ado." She was so small that her eyes were on a level with his, and he thought he saw her wink. "By the side door, you understand. That snooty lass on the desk is really too keen on the rules for my liking."

Patrick thrust the clock plans into her hand. "I'm sorry, but I broke the bird." The words came out more abruptly than he meant.

"Ah!" Her brow wrinkled. "Then how . . . ?"

"Patrick used *my* golf ball to fix the clock instead!" Danny burst out proudly. "It worked just as well." He paused and looked up at the small woman doubtfully. "Only it doesn't look as good," he admitted.

She nodded gravely at him. "I imagine not," she said. "Still, looks aren't everything. And I can have another bird made. Just exactly the same as the first."

"I thought it was *my* bird, you know," said Danny. He sighed. "I thought it was my prize. I found it. After Claire had found it. And then Eleanor Doon found it. And then I got it back. And then Patrick broke it." He sighed again. "It wasn't my real prize, but I liked it, the bird," he said. "It felt nice in my pocket."

"I imagine it did," said Anna Varga thoughtfully. She looked at their faces. "You look alike," she murmured. "Birds of a feather. And you have flocked together in this adventure, haven't you?"

They nodded, lost in her deep, black gaze.

"I am a lone bird by nature," the surprising woman added. "But this one time I needed help, and you gave it. I thank you for that, Patrick." She bowed to him.

Patrick blushed. He felt very uncomfortable.

Anna Varga straightened up, looked at him, and stroked her chin. "What do you suppose caused this upset?" she asked. Her eyes seemed to bore into him.

Patrick shuffled his feet and looked down. "Oh, I'm not quite sure," he muttered, awkwardly. Well, that's true in a way, he thought. Max did say we couldn't know for *sure* that Estelle's going back home actually caused the whole thing. Then he raised his eyes and looked straight at her. "I just know," he said clearly, "that it will never happen again."

"Ah," said Anna Varga. A small smile curved her lips. "Excellent. Well"—she pushed the clock plans into her handbag—"I must see to my clock. The golf ball will be returned to your little brother when the new regulator is made." She smiled at Danny. "I do hope your true prize comes to you in the end, young man." She nodded briskly, tucked the handbag under her arm, and trotted on up the ramp.

"She's a very polite lady, isn't she?" Danny remarked, looking after her.

"Weird, if you ask me." Claire shivered.

Patrick shook his head. *Odd beings, the clockmakers,* Max had said. He'd been right there. He looked at his brother and sister. "Let's go home," he said. "I want to show you something on my computer. I've got a feeling it'll work now."

At the bottom of the ramp Danny pounced on something with a yelp of joy. "My prize!" he yelled. "My prize! It came!" In his hand he held a shiny, stiff, faded black cap, with a silver badge. He put it on. It covered most of his face. "Cool!" he breathed, squinting up at them from under the shiny peak.

Patrick laughed. "Danny, that's not yours. Someone's lost that. Put it back!"

Danny's face fell.

"I don't think whoever lost it will be over here looking, really, Patrick," said Claire dreamily. She smiled to herself.

Patrick looked again at the cap and suddenly recognized it for what it was. He laughed, and Danny laughed, too, with relief.

"It *is* my prize, isn't it?" he shouted. "My prize! I got it! And Claire got a coat, didn't she? And a pretty hair thing, that I found for her. So that's her prize—" He hesitated. "But Patrick, you haven't got a prize. You didn't find anything, did you?"

Claire and Patrick looked at each other. It was better, really, that Danny didn't understand.

Then Patrick grinned. His prize? He looked at his brother and sister safe beside him, felt the sun on his face, breathed the warm air, glanced around at the familiar tree-lined streets, the slowly strolling Saturday shoppers. He thought of home, and his parents, and lunch, and his computer, even school on Monday. And while Danny watched him in astonishment, he stretched out his arms as if he could hug the whole thing.

"Finders keepers," he said.